"Cold?" Maks purred, pushing even closer. "Let me warm you."

"I'm not co—" But Gillian wasn't allowed to finish the thought.

His mouth covered hers in a kiss that demanded full submission and reciprocation.

Her body—the same body that had shied away from his every touch—now capitulated without a single conscious thought on her part. She sank into him while her mouth softened under his, allowing him immediate access to the interior.

Like the marauder his ancestors had been, he took advantage, his tongue seeking hers out with sensual intent. The hand on her throat slid down to her shoulder and then lower.

His triumphant growl was both animalistic and unbearably exciting.

This man might have all the urbanity expected of a prince on the outside, but underneath beat the heart of a ruthless Cossack. He wanted nothing less than *everything*.

BY HIS ROYAL DECREE

At his command and in his bed!

Crown Prince Maksim Yurkovich and his royal cousin
Prince Demyan know exactly the price of duty.

Having already sacrificed so much,
what is one more thing to them?

Tied to women by necessity, it's hard to say who is
more surprised by the fiery strength of their desire—
the Princes or their brides.

But when the sheets cool on the marriage bed
who will win…Queen or country?

Read Crown Prince Maksim's story this month in
ONE NIGHT HEIR

And next month discover how far Prince Demyan
will go to do his duty in
PRINCE OF SECRETS

ONE NIGHT HEIR

BY
LUCY MONROE

MILLS
BOON

First published in Great Britain 2013
by Mills & Boon, an imprint of Harlequin (UK) Limited.
Harlequin (UK) Limited, Eton House, 18-24 Paradise Road,
Richmond, Surrey TW9 1SR

© Lucy Monroe 2013

ISBN: 978 0 263 23500 5

ewable
stainable
) the

Lucy Monroe started reading at the age of four. After going through the childrens' books at home, she was caught by her mother reading adult novels pilfered from the higher shelves on the bookcase... Alas, it was nine years before she got her hands on a Mills & Boon® Romance her older sister had brought home. She loves to create the strong alpha males and independent women who people Mills & Boon® books. When she's not immersed in a romance novel (whether reading or writing it), she enjoys travel with her family, having tea with the neighbours, gardening, and visits from her numerous nieces and nephews.

Lucy loves to hear from her readers: e-mail LucyMonroe@LucyMonroe.com, or visit www.LucyMonroe.com

Recent titles by the same author:

NOT JUST THE GREEK'S WIFE
HEART OF A DESERT WARRIOR
FOR DUTY'S SAKE
THE GREEK'S PREGNANT LOVER

In sincerest gratitude to my readers,
who have stuck with me through the droughts brought
on by my mom's final illness and subsequent death,
my own health issues and the many other challenges
life offers us mortals. Your support and encouragement
mean so very much to me and have blessed me truly
beyond measure. Love and hugs to you all!

With particular thanks to Ms Gillian Wheatley of
London for suggesting visual inspiration for my hero.
XOXO

The necessary legal caveat: while Ms Wheatley shares
a first name with the female protagonist in this book,
Gillian Harris is not fashioned after her or based on
Ms Wheatley in any way. Any similarities are purely
coincidental and unintentional by the author.

CHAPTER ONE

FURY RIDING HIM like an angry stallion, Crown Prince Maksim of Volyarus let loose with a punch-cross-hook kickboxing combo against his cousin and sparring partner.

Demyan blocked, and the sound of flesh hitting pads mixed with his grunt of surprise. "Something the matter, your highness?"

Maks hated when his cousin, older by four years and raised as a brother with Maks in their family's palace, referred to him by his title.

Demyan was well aware, but the older man liked pushing buttons, especially during their workout sessions. He said it made the sparring more intense.

Today would have been sufficiently punishing without the added irritation. Not that Maks warned Demyan of that. His cousin deserved what he got.

"Nothing wiping the smug look off your face won't take care of." Maks danced back before driving forward with another fast-paced, grueling combo.

Well-matched in stature and strength, they both kept their six-feet-four-inch frames in top physical condition.

"I thought tonight was the big night with Gillian," Demyan said, scrambling in a way he rarely did during their sessions. "Don't tell me you think she's going to turn you down?"

"If I were going to ask, she'd say yes." And a day ago that certainty had given Maks a great deal of pleasure.

Now, it just taunted him with what he couldn't have. Namely, Gillian.

"So, what is the problem?" Demyan demanded as he went on the offensive, forcing Maks to defend against a barrage of punches and kicks.

"Her medical tests came back."

"She's not sick, is she?" Demyan asked, sounding sincerely concerned.

Coming from a man with a reputation for cold ruthlessness, it would have shocked anyone else.

But Maks knew how much Demyan cared about their family. And for the last eight months, the beautiful, sweet Gillian had been moving closer and closer to joining that group.

"She's perfectly fine." If you didn't count poorly functioning ovaries. "Now."

"What does that mean?"

"She had appendicitis when she was sixteen."

"That was ten years ago, what bearing does it have on her health now?"

"Fallopian tubes."

Demyan stopped and stared at Maks in confusion. "What?"

In no mood to give his cousin a break, Maks took

advantage of the other man's inattention and knocked him on his ass with a well-timed kick.

Demyan jumped to his feet, but he didn't come back for more like Maks expected. "Knock it off and explain what the hell appendicitis as a teenager has to do with an adult woman's fallopian tubes."

Demyan was no idiot. He knew Maks's interest in Gillian's reproductive system was of paramount importance to the House of Yurkovich, the royal family of Volyarus.

"She has a poorly functioning reproductive system." Maks adjusted his thin sparring gloves. "There is less than a thirty percent chance of pregnancy."

A lot less by some estimations, slightly more by others, according the specialist Maks had consulted.

Demyan shoved hair the same dark color as Maks's own off his forehead. "With fertility treatment?"

"I have no intention of becoming the next father of sextuplets."

"Don't be an ass."

"I'm not. You know I cannot marry a woman who won't be able to produce the next heir plus a spare."

Demyan didn't reply immediately. They were both too personally aware of the costs associated with those issues.

"You aren't your father. You don't have to marry a woman you don't love in order to provide an heir."

"I have no intention of doing so. Neither will I marry a woman I like whose only hope of providing that child would be via often painful and not always successful fertility treatments."

"You could adopt."

"Like my parents adopted you?"

"They didn't formally adopt me. I am still a Zaretsky. It was never your father's intention that I inherit the throne."

"You were just his spare," Maks muttered with some bitterness.

Demyan shrugged. "Duty is duty."

"And my duty precludes asking Gillian Harris to marry me." His personal sense of honor also dictated he break things off with her as soon as possible.

"You don't love her?" Demyan asked with only mild curiosity.

"You know better."

"Love only leads to pain," Demyan quoted one of Maks's mother's favorite refrains.

Maks added the rest. "And a compromise on duty."

Both men had reason to believe it, too.

"What are you going to do?" Demyan asked, dropping back into a sparring stance.

Maks executed a simple forward jab-left hook combo. "What do you think?"

"I'll miss her."

Maks didn't doubt it. One of the reasons he'd decided to ask Gillian to marry him was that despite her mostly small-town upbringing, she got along surprisingly well with his family and successfully navigated social situations many would find overwhelming.

The daughter of a renowned world news correspondent, Gillian had been attending events with the world's richest and most powerful since a young age.

Demyan blocked Maks's kick and returned one of his own. "Are you going to tell her tonight?"

"I may not need to." The lovely blue-eyed blonde would have gotten a copy of the results of her latest physical.

Gillian would know about the reasons behind her irregular menses now as well. She already knew the responsibilities associated with his position. She should be expecting the dissolution of their relationship.

A more practical woman than most, he had hopes there would be no awkward "breakup" scene.

"Yes, Nana, I think tonight's the night," Gillian said into the phone mashed to her ear with her shoulder as she hopped around the room trying to get her shoes on.

"Has he told you he loved you yet?" Evelyn Harris, Gillian's nana and the woman who had raised her, asked.

"No."

"Your grandfather has told me every night before we go to sleep for the last forty-eight years that he loves me."

"I know, Nana." But Maks was different.

He held his emotions in check like it was a royal imperative, and ever the dutiful prince, he obeyed. They came out when he was making love, though. After a fashion.

Maks made love with the single-minded intensity of a man who was thinking of nothing else but pleasing and getting lost in the woman who shared his bed.

For the past seven months, that woman had been Gillian.

They'd dated a month before he took her to bed the first time. She'd found that odd at the time, considering his reputation, but later she'd realized that, as unbelievable as it might seem, Maks was looking for more from her than a casual bed partner.

And while she'd been more thrilled than shocked, she'd been stunned all the same.

She didn't belong in his circle. She was not rich, famous, or powerful, but Gillian's father still liked to see her when he was in town. That inevitably meant going to some function or other on his arm. He couldn't dedicate time simply to visiting her, so he included Gillian in his schedule.

As the famous news correspondent's unremarkable daughter, Gillian had attended more than her fair share of diplomatic and high society events.

No one had been more shocked than she when it turned out that Crown Prince Maksim Yurkovich of Volyarus seemed to *like* unremarkable. Several comments made by him, and a couple by his mother on the few occasions Gillian had met the queen, had made it clear that royalty did not look for notoriety when choosing a mate.

Though regardless, she would have thought Maks would be looking for someone with more personal cache than Gillian to bring into the royal family. Apparently Volyarussians did not have the same requirements for pedigree in a mate than other royal families of the world.

And there couldn't be anyone less notorious than the small-town girl from Alaska who made her living as what her father termed a "chocolate-box" photographer.

There was nothing objectionable, or even questionable in Gillian's past. Her parents hadn't stayed together and neither had been interested in raising her, but they'd entered into a short businesslike marriage prior to her birth and hadn't filed for divorce until a year after.

"I may as well hang up now, your mind is clearly in the clouds again, child," Nana said over the phone line.

Gillian shoved her blond hair behind her ear and adjusted the phone. "I'm sorry, Nana. I didn't mean to—"

"I know. You get to thinking about Maks and the rest of your brain shuts off, especially the part attached to your ears."

"It's not that bad."

Her grandmother's snort said the older woman did not agree. "You make that boy tell you that he loves you before you agree to be his wife."

"He's hardly a boy, Nana." Gillian had made the same protest before, but to little effect.

"I'm seventy-five years old, Gillian. He's a boy to me."

"Some people never say those words," Gillian pointed out, returning to the subject she knew her grandmother considered most important.

"Some people have less sense than God gave a gnat then."

"Rich doesn't say it, but he loves me." Even as she said the words, Gillian knew she wasn't actually certain that they were *true.*

Her father wasn't an affectionate or demonstrative man. Rich Harris had made little more than a moderate effort to be part of her life, but he'd also been the one to make sure she had two people to raise her who loved and cared for her. The two dear people who had raised him.

"Your daddy is an idiot, no matter what those Pulitzer Prize people say."

Gillian laughed, knowing her grandmother didn't mean the words. Nana was hugely proud of her world famous son and still held out the hope that one day he would take on the role of Gillian's father.

That ship had sailed a long time ago, but Gillian would never say so to the older woman.

She owed too much to Nana to hurt her in any way. "Don't you let him hear you say that. He'll take back the motor home."

"I'd like to see him try. I still have a wooden spoon and I'm not afraid to use it."

Gillian couldn't help more laughter at that. Nana'd had the same fabled wooden spoon all the years of her growing up, too, but her backside had never felt the flat side of it.

"I swear, I don't know what makes that boy of mine think like he does."

"He's fine, Nana. His dreams didn't include having a family. That doesn't make him bad."

"Well, he has a daughter, whether he dreamed you up or not."

"I know." She'd spent her whole life knowing that while she had not been precisely wanted, both her parents had given her the gift of life and that was as far as the sacrifice was ever going to go.

"I don't like to see you settling," Nana said in that tone Gillian hated.

It was the I-worry-about-you-child-I-really-do tone and it came five minutes before Nana decided she needed to give up whatever adventure she and Papa were on to fly back to Seattle and check in on her granddaughter.

"I'm fine, Nana. Better than fine." She was on the verge of getting engaged to the man she loved with her whole heart. "I don't need the words."

And she didn't. She needed the actions. She needed Maks to put her first, to treat her like she mattered and he did that. His life was both high-profile and extremely busy, but Maks didn't cancel dates, he didn't show up late, and he didn't dismiss her interests or her career as a studio photographer.

"Hmmph."

That sound was almost as concerning as the older woman's tone earlier. It implied that Nana would be having a talk with Maks.

Gillian sighed. The man would have to be strong

enough to withstand a talking-to, or ten, if they were going to be married.

"Are you and Papa enjoying Vegas?" she asked, hoping to turn to the topic.

"He lost money at the blackjack tables, but I won on the slots." The glee in her grandmother's tone brought a smile to Gillian's face.

"Is Rich still meeting you two for dinner next week?"

"He hasn't *texted* us to cancel." Nana's lack of fondness for texting came through in the way she said the word.

"Good."

"I suppose we'll have good news to tell him."

"I think so." The doorbell rang. "That's him, I've got to go."

"You call us tomorrow, you hear?"

"Yes, Nana." With news.

Smiling, Gillian rushed to answer the door summons. Her gaze fell on the manila envelope with the results from her latest physical. She hadn't read it yet, but didn't expect anything surprising.

Gillian had her physical yearly, something her father had insisted on since she'd nearly died from appendicitis at the age of sixteen. She chose to see it as proof of affection he never gave voice to.

Maks looked serious and devastatingly attractive in his black Armani suit as Gillian pulled the door open.

She smiled up at all six feet four inches of muscular male towering confidently in her doorway. "You're early."

"And yet you are ready. You are no ordinary woman, Gillian Harris." He didn't return her smile, but his espresso-brown eyes traveled down her body like a caress.

He always did that, making her feel like all the super models in the world wouldn't take his attention from her decidedly normal blond hair, blue eyes, average height and curves.

She stepped back to let him in. "Nana didn't stand for tardiness."

"And here I believed you were so eager to see me, you could not wait to get dressed," he teased.

She grinned up at him. "That, too."

He lowered his head and kissed her, his lips brushing hers in polite greeting. She returned the kiss, letting her mouth open just slightly because she liked the feel of their breath mingling.

He made an inarticulate sound and deepened the kiss, pulling her body flush to his as he maneuvered them back into her apartment. As so often happened when they kissed, time stopped moving for her and the only thing her consciousness registered was the feel of his lips on hers and his hard body so close.

When he pulled back, they were both breathing a little heavily.

His dark gaze fell to the manila envelope by the door. She'd opened it, but the phone call had come in from Nana before she could skim the contents. She wasn't worried, though. At twenty-six, she was young. She lived a healthy lifestyle and showed no signs of illness.

Nana would chastise her nonetheless. It was a good thing the older woman was in Las Vegas.

"You got your results." There was a curiously flat quality to Maks's tone.

She nodded and led the way into the living room. "Would you like something to drink before we go?"

"I'll take a shot of Old Pulteney, if you have it."

"You know I do." She'd kept the twenty-one-year-old single malt whiskey on hand since he'd admitted to it being his drink of choice.

Gillian poured Maks two fingers in a rock glass, no ice, and handed it over.

"Thank you." He took a larger sip than usual.

She smiled, charmed by the evidence of nervousness in a man so completely self-assured.

"You never told me you had appendicitis when you were sixteen."

"You never asked." He'd seen the scar, faded and small though it was.

She was surprised it had been mentioned in her health report, though. His doctor had obviously done a much more thorough examination than her own GP for this physical. She wasn't surprised in the least that Maks had read the report with such attention to detail, though.

That was very much like him.

Maks frowned and took a sip of his drink.

Not sure why having had appendicitis was worth a frown, Gillian poured club soda over ice and added a slice of lime, her drink of choice. Maybe Maks was like her father and responded strongly to the knowledge she'd almost died.

When Rich visited her in the hospital, it was the one and only time Gillian had seen overt concern for her on his movie star handsome face.

Her father never appreciated the reminder that he'd been vulnerable to worry for her and she assumed Maks would be the same, so she didn't comment on it, but asked instead, "Where are we going for dinner?"

He'd said he wanted to take her somewhere special. Combined with the fact he'd asked for the results of her yearly physical and that his own GP perform it, she was pretty confident that tonight was supposed to end in a proposal.

One she had no intention of turning down.

She loved him wholly and completely. She'd never told him, either. She hadn't admitted *that* to Nana, but the words had turned out surprisingly difficult for Gillian to utter.

"Chez Rennet."

It was the first restaurant he'd ever taken her to. No, he hadn't said the words, but Maks had a romantic streak he wasn't that great at hiding.

"Terrific. I love Rennet's food." The chef and owner had a soft spot for both her and Maks as well.

Dining in his restaurant was always pleasurable and Gillian took that as further evidence Maks wanted tonight to be special.

"I know you do." Again that serious look.

And it finally clicked. Tonight *was* a serious night,

an evening that would culminate in the kind of conversation she was sure Maks only planned to have once in his life.

She hadn't been nervous before, but knowing how important tonight was to him brought a flock of humming birds to take up residence inside Gillian.

She was getting engaged to a prince, and for the first time, she really thought about what it would be like to be a princess.

The prospect was more than a little daunting.

Nana had always said Gillian ignored what she did not want to deal with and she'd done a fair job of that while dating Maks, but his somber demeanor tonight forced her to evaluate what his proposal would mean to both of them.

Ultimately, however, it didn't matter.

She would have given up the creature comforts of civilization and moved to Antarctica to be with him.

Taking on the role of princess and living at least half the year in the Baltic island country of Volyarus would not be allowed to frighten her.

She loved him, Maks the man.

She could and would live with Maksim of the House of Yurkovich, Crown Prince of Volyarus.

CHAPTER TWO

DINNER WAS WONDERFUL. Although the solemn air never left Maks, he charmed Gillian with his usual urbanity.

There were several times he seemed on the verge of discussing something important, but he never followed through.

This further proof of a nervousness she never would have expected beguiled Gillian. She found herself falling just that much more in love with the man of her dreams as the evening wore on.

After dinner, he took her to listen to live jazz, one of her favorite things. The band was made up of musicians who had been around long enough they understood the music and how to live it, not just play it.

Relaxing, she was even relieved that the music prevented discussion, and the odd pressure she'd felt Maks was under seemed to lighten.

Afterward, she asked him back to her apartment and as expected, he accepted.

He'd taken her coat and laid it over the back of one of her club chairs, but stood as if not knowing what came next. It was so unlike him that she took pity and suggested another drink.

"I'd better not."

"You don't have to drive. Not if you don't want to." She offered her bed for the night in a similar oblique fashion to how she'd done on numerous occasions before.

He usually took her up on it, only refusing when he had early morning meetings or travel plans that would require him leaving in the wee hours and disturbing her rest.

So, it surprised her when he hesitated now. "Do you think that's a good idea?"

Did he think she wanted to spend less time with him with marriage in the offing? She wasn't going to pretend sexual innocence for the tabloids once their relationship went public. Though she appreciated the fact he'd kept it under wraps thus far, at some point in the very near future, everyone would know about them.

And she did not mind, but she would not pretend, either.

"Yes," she said firmly.

"We need to talk."

"After." Suddenly she knew she wanted words of love spoken between them, even if they only came from her before he proposed.

She would tell him while they made love. He could propose after.

Yearning she would not think of denying darkened his espresso gaze. "You are certain this is a good idea?"

"Yes." She wasn't sure where the need came from, but she could not bear the thought of agreeing to marry him without admitting her feelings for him.

If only with her body, then so be it, but she would express her love for him tonight and she had hope the words would make it past her lips as well.

Need did not make those three small words any easier to say. She could no more simply blurt them out than she could dance naked on a table at *Chez Rennet.*

While her grandparents had told Gillian they loved her and accepted the words in return, it wasn't daily like her nana claimed her papa did with her. And Gillian had only ever said the words to her own parents when she was younger.

Neither had ever returned them and she could not remember the last time she'd had the courage to speak her love for the absentee adults in her life. She'd never spoken them to another man, but then she'd never been in love before, either. Her heart wasn't so easy to reach.

With Maks, she had the option of showing him physically what she felt so strongly emotionally. He would *know* she loved him at the end of this night. One way or another.

He shook his head. "You are a very different sort of woman, aren't you?"

She didn't think so, but she liked the way he looked at her like she was something special, so she didn't deny it. And really, wasn't he supposed to think she was extraordinary? Their future would be rather grim if she was just like any other woman to him.

She certainly considered Maks a man above all others.

Maks took her hand and tugged her toward the hall that led to her bedroom. "Come. I have a mind to make love to you in comfort."

They'd been intimate in the living room many times, but she didn't mind him considering this time important and special. Maybe he found the words just as difficult to speak, but this was his way of showing how much he cared, too.

Regardless of his reasoning, her heart beat a rapid rhythm as she let him lead her into the darkened bedroom. Maks dropped her hand before crossing to the small table and turning on the lamp. Made of bronze and fashioned like a statue, the clump of three calla lilies had bulbs in each of the glass flowers that cast a soft golden glow over the room.

He'd given her the painting of a blonde woman standing with her head bowed in a field of the same blooms hanging on the wall above it. Maks had said it reminded him of her.

She thought the painting far too ethereal to have her likeness, but she loved it.

He turned to face her now, his chiseled features set in somber lines. "You give me a great gift." He sighed, releasing some great burden. "I needed this."

She smiled, her emotions choking her but still not rising to her lips to say aloud.

He seemed to understand because he came back to her and pulled her into a passionate kiss that let them both get lost for a little while. They were breathing heavily when their mouths separated and she was wrapped securely in his arms.

"You are a very good kisser."

"Or you are," he teased, more like his normal self.

"You're the one with all the experience." She hadn't been a virgin when they met, but she might as well have been for all her experience.

Two different fumbling attempts during her university days at intimacy that ended in dismal failure and none of the pleasure she found in his arms had left her with no real practical experience at pleasing a partner.

Maks had never minded and had always been extremely patient and *happy even* to teach her the joys of two bodies coming together when real attraction existed on both sides.

"We are good together like this." He sounded almost sad about that.

But he had nothing to be sad about, so she had to be misreading that tone in his voice. Or was he one of those men who believed that marriage meant sex went by the wayside?

She'd show him otherwise if he was.

She was a twenty-first-century woman who believed that not only were women *supposed* to enjoy sex, but that it belonged very firmly and frequently in the marriage bed.

She didn't say any of that, but concentrated on divesting him of his suit. He helped by toeing off his shoes and socks and yanking his dress shirt over his head once his tie had been loosened and the top few buttons undone.

"Eager, aren't you?" she teased.

"You have no idea." He nearly ripped her dress getting it off, her bra and panties disappearing with none of his usual finesse or time spent on visual appreciation for her preference for matching lace.

They were naked moments later. He looked at her then, his brown eyes eating her up with hot hunger.

She could feel her body's response to that look, her nipples tightening even more than they already were, her inner walls contracting with the need to be filled by his hard sex.

Heat suffused her from her toes all the way up her limbs, sending a blush of desire over her cheeks and shivers of emotionally laced physical need quaking through her.

They'd barely touched and she wanted sex with this man in this moment more than she'd ever wanted anything or another man, Maks included. Knowing this intimacy was the prelude of a lifetime together increased her passion in ways she would never have expected.

The expression in his eyes said he was similarly affected. Maks looked desperate with his need to be with her.

Without thought, she stepped into his arms and it felt so right when he lifted her like a bride and carried her to the bed. He managed to yank back the covers and top sheet without dropping her.

She helped by wrapping her arms around his neck.

Not so helpful were the small, exploratory kisses she placed along his jaw and down his neck. She stopped to inhale where his neck met his shoulder.

The subtle fragrance of his Armani cologne mixed with his own masculine scent triggering a reflexive response in Gillian's core that she could not stop, even if she had wanted to. And she didn't.

She loved the feel of her body preparing itself for his possession, reveled in the reaction that was primal and visceral to things like his smell and as simple a touch as his hand brushing down her hip as he laid her on the mattress.

"You are all that I want," he whispered in her ear. "If only…"

She didn't know if only what. In that moment, could not begin to care. His hands were moving over her, bringing her pleasure unlike anything she'd ever known.

Even at his touch.

There was such profundity in that moment, she did not see how their wedding night could possibly be any better or more special.

She touched him, too, mapping his body with her hands, loving the feel of his muscles, the tickle of his chest hair against her fingertips.

This amazing man, who was literally a prince and business tycoon rolled into one, belonged to her and as difficult as she might find that to believe, the proof was in her position. Naked, in bed with him, free to caress his masculine body as she liked.

"You and Demyan keep yourselves in amazing shape," she opined happily.

Maks's face twisted at the mention of his cousin's name. Another time she would have asked about that, but not tonight.

What they were doing was too important. What she was doing was life-altering, especially if she could force those three all-important words out of her voice box.

"Our sparring was rough today," Maks said, as if he realized she might wonder at his reaction.

She brushed her fingertip over a bruise she'd just noticed. "It looks like it."

"That is nothing," Maks said with his typical arrogance and pride that would never admit Demyan may have gotten the better of him in the sparring ring.

His cousin was hard to get to know, but the older man and Maks were close. She liked knowing he had a friend he could trust. Maks didn't live in a world where trust or even trustworthiness came in great supply. Gillian understood that world; she'd been on the edges of it because of her father for her whole life.

She leaned forward and kissed the discolored skin, then the area all around it.

Maks groaned. "I like."

She knew he did. He loved being pampered, even in bed. He gave as good as he got, though, so she never minded giving either.

He rolled her onto her back and came over her, his big body covering hers both sensually and protectively.

Maks looked down into her eyes, his own dark with emotion. "You are so perfect for me. Too perfect."

She just shook her head. Didn't he know there could be no too much about it?

He kissed her like he didn't want to discuss it. Like he couldn't bear not kissing her one more second. Like she belonged to him wholly and completely.

She kissed him back with her heart on her lips, because she did.

He pressed her into the mattress, the kiss going on and on and on, increasing intensity with every passing minute until the fire blazing between them was plasma hot.

All thought and feeling outside the pleasure their bodies brought to one another disintegrated in its path.

Wanting him inside her, *now,* Gillian spread her legs in invitation.

Instead of accepting, Maks moved back, breaking the kiss. "Not yet."

"Yes," she demanded.

But he shook his head, the expression in his eyes both feral and intense. He began to touch her again, this time with the clear and express purpose of driving her insane with delight.

He found the spot on her foot that made her shiver with need and the area of her inner thigh that made her ache to be filled. He caressed the curve of her waist and moved up to give careful attention to her breasts, licking and laving, kneading and playing until her nipples hurt with the need to be touched, too.

Only then did he put his mouth over one engorged tip and bite lightly.

She cried out, a mini orgasm going off inside her.

He let out a dark chuckle and sucked her nipple while her body writhed under him of its own volition. He pinched her other nipple between his thumb and forefinger before brushing it featherlightly with his thumb. He did this over and over again as she moaned for more.

She was begging with her body and a few inarticulate "Pleases" by the time he pressed her thighs wide and surged inside her without a condom for the first time.

The thought they could be making a child increased her ecstasy to the point that her entire body convulsed with climax on his first initial thrust.

He didn't slow down and she didn't ask him to. He kept surging in and out of her, building pleasure that never actually slipped into lassitude until she came for the second time, her contractions so harsh, the rigidity of her body thrust him upward.

He never lost his position inside her, though, and shouted with pure male triumph when he came.

He looked down at her, his expression so intent, it sent aftershocks quivering through her. "Thank you."

She shook her head, no words coming out. Not even the three she wanted so badly to say, but then maybe they weren't necessary. After that, he had to know how she felt. She had no doubts about his feelings for her. A man could not make love to a woman with that level of passion and feel none of the finer emotions.

"I should have asked. About the condom."

"No. It's all right." They didn't need barriers between them.

He nodded, his expression somber as he moved to
lie beside her. "I would like to spend the night. May I?"

"Yes." She wasn't sure why he felt the need to ask,
but then maybe it was that kind of moment.

So much, it deserved proper consideration.

Gillian woke wrapped in Maks's strong arms. She could
tell by his breathing that he was already awake.

Suddenly the words that had been impossible to utter
were on the tip of her tongue. She sat up and looked at
him in the morning light diffused by her bedroom cur-
tains. "I love you, Maks."

How easy had that been? The words had practically
said themselves, but she found she wasn't comfortable
maintaining eye contact. Particularly when his were
showing evidence of shock at her announcement.

How could he not have known? How could her words
possibly come as a surprise to him after everything?
Or was it her timing?

She'd never uttered those words to another man,
didn't know if there were protocols in Maks's world
that dictated they get said after morning greetings.

That sounded ridiculous, but it wouldn't be the first
aspect to the life of a royal that she found so. It was a
good thing she did love him, or she'd never consider
spending her life in that kind of weirdly orchestrated
fishbowl.

She tucked back down into bed, snuggling against him. "I could get used to this."

"It is too bad we cannot."

She heard the words, but they didn't make sense, so they didn't register.

Her mind was still on the night before and how unburdened she felt after making her confession this morning. Even if it had been awkwardly done.

At least he hadn't laughed at her.

That was one of the nice things about Maks. He never mocked another person's lack of aplomb, even though he never seemed short of suaveness.

"Last night was amazing," she offered.

"Yes." His tone was so serious and almost unhappy.

She didn't understand why.

Maybe he was tired. He had been very energetic throughout the night. Honestly, she wasn't sure she'd survive if every night was as passionate as the one before, wonderful as it had been.

They hadn't gone to sleep after the first time making love, but had come together three more times throughout the night. Maks had never been so insatiable. She'd never felt such freedom to respond.

He'd been voracious, both for touching her and being inside of her. And she'd loved every second of it.

Her body twinged delightfully at the reminders of how hungry he had been.

"I am sorry." If anything, Maks's tone had grown heavier.

As much as she'd prefer to pretend she didn't know why he'd apologized, she could not.

But she *could* tell him that it didn't matter. She didn't need Maks to admit love for her so long as he needed her like he'd shown he did the night before.

"It's all right." Gingerly, keeping a lid on her own disappointment, Gillian sat up and met Maks's gaze.

His expression was stoic, like a man trying to pretend something didn't bother him. "No. Last night was a mistake, I think."

Then he winced as if he realized he should not have said that.

And well he might wince, the idiot. She wasn't going to demand words of love, but downplaying the night before wasn't going to fly with her, either.

Suddenly she had a thought that might explain his odd attitude. "You want to pretend we don't have sex?"

And did that bother him as much as she thought it did? As much as it absolutely appalled her?

"As wonderful as we are together, it will not be a pretense. It cannot. It would not be fair to you, or to me, if I am honest."

Her brows drew together. "I don't understand. You want to stop having sex?"

Until they were married? A royal wedding required at least a year, often two to prepare for. No wonder he'd been so hungry the night before.

But why forego condoms? Did he hope to have gotten her pregnant so they were forced to marry more quickly?

That just didn't seem like something Maks would do. He was not a master of passive aggressive. Full-on aggression was more his style.

"Continuing to have sex together will only make our eventual breakup all the harder, not to mention increasing the chances of the media picking up on our relationship. We've been lucky so far, they've left us alone."

Gillian thought that had something to do with her father's influence as much as how circumspect she and Maks had been. But that wasn't the most important thing right now.

"Break up?" she asked, completely at a loss. "Why would we break up?"

They were getting married. Weren't they? A cold spike of dread pierced her heart. *Weren't they?*

His expression was not hope producing. "A breakup between us is inevitable. Surely you understand this."

CHAPTER THREE

"No. Pretend my IQ is in the low digits and explain it to me." Gillian's throat felt tight, the words hard to get out.

"I cannot marry a woman incapable of providing heirs to the throne. It's draconian, I know, but nevertheless, it is the way things must be."

"I can't provide heirs to the throne?" she asked, still very confused, but with a growing sense of apprehension that was making her current circumstances—naked and in bed with him—increasingly uncomfortable.

He frowned, sitting up, seemingly unconcerned by *his* nudity as he made no effort to cover himself. "You said you'd read the results of your physical."

"I said I'd received it. I had."

"I saw the envelope. It was opened."

"Nana called before I skimmed the results."

"One would think on something so important, one might do more than *skim*." His speech only grew so formal when he was very annoyed.

What did he have to be angry about?

"I've been healthy since my appendicitis at sixteen."

"The surgery to keep you alive left your fallopian

tubes compromised," Maks said with the air of a man
who did not like having to explain himself.

Compromised fallopian tubes? What the heck did
that mean?

Unable to stand the false sense of intimacy their situation provided once second longer, she jumped out of
the bed. Grabbing her robe, she yanked it on so hard
she wouldn't have been surprised if the sleeve ripped
right off.

Gillian stepped back from the bed, putting as much
distance as possible between herself and Maks while
staying in the same room. "What are you talking
about?"

Once again, Maks looked pained. "The likelihood
of you getting pregnant is very low."

"What about fertility treatments?" Or had he not
even considered them?

She was defective and therefore not worthy to be his
bride. *Oh, God.* The silent prayer was filled with anguish, but received no heavenly reply.

Last night had not been about hunger or passion. It
had been about saying good-bye. Everything she'd taken
to mean they belonged together was in fact supposed
to indicate the opposite.

"Fertility treatment could be an option for you with
someone else," he said, like he was offering her good
news.

"But not you."

"Marrying you knowing we would have to use them

would not be an intelligent or well thought out move on the part of our House."

"I would not be marrying your *House,*" she practically shouted.

She wouldn't be marrying anyone. Pain at that realization nearly took her to her knees.

What all this *talk* meant was that she was losing Maks.

"That is not true. I am a prince who will one day be king. I was born to a burden of duty none but elected officials in country can begin to understand. And even they live in their roles only temporarily whereas I will never know a day when my small country does not have to come first and foremost in my thinking."

She knew that. One of the few truly ruling monarchies left in the world, as Crown Prince of Volyarus, Maks's life was not his own. But his choices were.

"You do not love me." It was the only thing that really mattered and incidentally made absolute sense of his unwillingness to pursue fertility options.

He liked her, he desired her, he might even be as sad as he appeared at first over breaking up with her, but he *did not love her.*

"Love is not an emotion I have the freedom or inclination to pursue."

"Love either is, or *is not.* You don't have to pursue it." She'd learned as a small child, no matter how hard you *tried,* you could not make someone love you.

No. Love could not be forced. Nor could it be denied. Though she would give up her next visit with her grandparents and any hope of ever seeing either of her biological parents again if she could deny the tidal wave of emotions threatening to drown her now.

"You said you love me. I am sorry." Genuine regret reflected in the espresso depths of his eyes.

That regret hurt her as much as the words that came with it because the remorse proved their sincerity. Pain was a vise around her heart, radiating through her body in an unexpected and equally undeniable physical reaction to the emotional blow.

She could barely breathe for the agony. It was by sheer will she remained on her feet.

He was *sorry.*

She wanted to cry, felt like screaming, but she held it all in along with the pain building toward nuclear meltdown.

"Get out." She spoke quietly, but she knew he heard her.

"You are not thinking rationally."

"Since our first date, you've been very careful to keep us out of the eyes of the media."

"Yes."

She didn't ask, "Why?" Didn't really care about his reasoning anymore.

She just wanted him gone so she could let the pain out. *He* didn't get to see it.

"Do you think me calling the building's security to have you removed from my apartment would blow all those efforts to hell?"

His eyes widened at her oblique threat. "You're not going to call security."

He really didn't know her as well as he thought he did.

She spun around and pressed the panic button on her bedroom's security box.

"You have about a minute, maybe two, before they arrive. If you want to be caught here, by all means, stay." She didn't turn to face him as she spoke and she didn't raise her voice, either.

If she did, she'd end up screaming. She just knew it. And Gillian had never screamed a day in her life. She wasn't going to start now.

Not with him.

Not when the anguish inside her was already so close to imploding and taking her heart with it.

Ukrainian curses sounded along with the brush of clothing being yanked over naked limbs.

He paused at the doorway. She could sense it, though hadn't turned to watch his departure.

"I *am* sorry." Then he was gone.

And she was alone. Unable to stand under the on-slaught of emotional agony ripping through her, Gillian sank to the floor.

Every dream she'd nursed in the past months shattered, every hope she'd let herself entertain despite her past and present life that in no way matched his for brilliance ripped violently from her still bleeding heart.

* * *

Nine weeks later, dazed and disbelieving, Gillian sat on the park bench outside her doctor's offices.

Utterly shattered by the news she'd received, she could do little more than stare at the tall buildings surrounding the small patch of nature.

Her doctor's words seemed impossible. *"You're pregnant."*

It was terribly improbable. And yet it was true.

She was pregnant. Exactly nine weeks along.

One night of unprotected sex with a man intent on evicting her from his life and they'd made a baby.

Emotions she had spent two months trying to contain and stifle were rioting through her. For the first time in her life, she was completely unable to ignore what she did not want to face.

Okay, maybe for the second.

Her grief over Maks's rejection had been so consuming, Gillian had no chance at ignoring it, either. Each day was a new reminder how much she'd loved, how much she'd lost and how much she missed the jerk.

But she'd worked toward some semblance of peace. She could almost sleep through the night without waking from a nightmare into the one of loss.

Pain at Maks's rejection had simply become such a part of her, she hardly noticed it anymore.

Or so she told herself.

It was the hope she couldn't stand. The need to feel anything at all, but most of all love for another human being, even a very tiny one.

Because unlike her parents, Gillian didn't care how her pregnancy had come to be. Planned or unplanned. With someone she wanted to share a life, or alone. None of it mattered.

She *would* love her child, already did, from the moment her doctor had uttered those impossible words, even before Gillian had been *sure.*

She had insisted they do the test again. Her doctor's PA had drawn Gillian's blood, but then she'd gone one step further while they waited for the in-office lab to run the results of the second test. She'd brought out a small device called a Doppler. A mini-ultrasound, the PA used the Doppler to find the baby's heartbeat.

Gillian had cried and nearly fainted when she heard the fast paced *swoosh-swoosh-swoosh* through the handheld device. There could be no denying another being was growing inside her womb. Her baby.

Maks's baby.

Unsurprisingly, at that point, the second test had come back just as conclusively positive as the first.

Gillian's pregnancy appeared perfectly viable, though her doctor wasn't particularly pleased about the fact she'd lost enough weight to hollow her cheeks. She'd been quick to assure Gillian this wasn't as uncommon as people might believe, however.

Many women lost weight in their first trimester.

Even so, miscarriage rates were higher than Gillian had ever expected. According to her doctor's PA, one in five pregnancies ended in miscarriage.

Wasn't that horrifically high for a country with such advanced medical knowledge and care?

Despite the early summer sun beating down, Gillian's hands were cold and clammy.

Pregnant. *Her.*

Part of her mind vaguely realized she was in shock. She probably should have stayed in the exam cubicle, but Gillian had needed to get out into the fresh air.

So, she'd told the doctor she was fine and the woman was busy enough to let her leave without pushing further.

Gillian shook her head, everything about the last hour incomprehensible.

She'd made an appointment to see her doctor at Nana's insistence. Gillian hadn't been all that concerned. She'd fought a serious case of depression since kicking Maks out of her apartment nine weeks before.

She loved him and saying the words had only made that knowledge more awful to bear when she'd realized there was no way he returned the feelings.

She'd *thought* she had a really persistent flu for the last few weeks, and frankly hadn't much cared. If her grandparents hadn't come into town for a visit, Gillian might well not have realized she was pregnant until she started showing.

But Nana had been very upset when she'd gotten Gillian to admit she had felt lethargic and nauseated for *weeks.* Though she'd only thrown up a few times.

According to Gillian's doctor, she was lucky in that.

The woman had also evinced surprise at Gillian not realizing there was even a possibility she was pregnant.

After all, she hadn't had a period in three months, but then Gillian's cycle had never been regular. Skipping a month was not unusual.

Compromised fallopian tubes, but they weren't compromised enough. Not only had Gillian managed to fall pregnant the one and only time she'd ever made love without a condom, but she'd been in the wrong part of her cycle for it to happen, too.

It was a miracle really.

She wondered if Maks would see the baby growing inside her that way? Most likely not. He'd walked away from her much too easily to be pleased when she popped up before him, carrying his child.

Would he even believe her that the baby was his? She wasn't risking miscarriage doing an amniocentesis for the DNA test.

No way was she.

If he had doubts about his fatherhood, he could wait until after the birth to assuage them.

As much as they would undoubtedly love the baby when it was born, Gillian's pregnancy wasn't going to make her grandparents happy. They firmly believed sex and pregnancy belonged within the bounds of marriage.

It only took a second to consider before she knew hiding her condition from them for the few days they were supposed to be in Seattle would be the best course of action.

There was a twenty percent chance this pregnancy

wouldn't make it past the first trimester. Gillian wasn't telling *anyone* about it until she'd made it past that important time marker.

Which meant she'd better turn in an Academy Award nominee worthy performance of a woman feeling one hundred percent better. Or her grandparents wouldn't be leaving town and heading for Canada the middle of next week as planned.

She would tell them her doctor said she was a little run down and needed to take better vitamins. It was the truth, if not the whole truth. Gillian's GP had prescribed gummy prenatal vitamins, which were supposed to be easier on her sensitive stomach, and folic acid for improved fetal development.

She'd also suggested an iron supplement because Gillian's levels were on the low end. That, at least, was a better explanation of her fatigue than the one she'd come up with on her own.

Missing Maks was exhausting.

Her grandparents would have no trouble accepting that Gillian wasn't feeling completely up to par in general. They believed the breakup had taken its toll on Gillian's health and hadn't hesitated to say so. Gillian had reminded them that most women had their heart broken at least once by the time they were her age.

Many had even been married and divorced by the age of twenty-six.

Nana had harrumphed and commented several times that she thought, "That young man had a lot to answer for."

It was a good thing Gillian's first appointment with her obstetrician wasn't until the following Friday, though. She didn't want to tell her grandparents another half-truth if she could help it.

Maks barked an answer into his phone and then cut the connection without saying goodbye.

"Idiots," he grumbled under his breath.

Demyan said from the doorway, "It seems everyone we do business with has lost IQ points in the last months."

Maks took a deep breath and consciously reined in his initial urge to snap at his cousin. "Did you need something, Demyan?"

"I have some information I believe you will find very interesting."

"We don't need another outlet for the rare minerals mines. We cannot keep up with demand as it is." Not and maintain environmental integrity.

A must for any energy or mineral extraction endeavor for Volyarus companies. Maks's father and grandfather before him had been well ahead of times in protecting the earth for future generations. No country on earth had stricter environmental regulations and policies than Volyarus.

And Yurkovich Tanner was ahead of any of the big ten oil companies in developing alternative energy sources as well.

As CEO, it was Maks's job to make sure that continued to be the case. "The last time I checked, our wind farm productions are all on schedule, too."

"It's not about business."

"I already know Father and the countess are on a *secret* getaway in the Cayman Islands." Maks made no effort to curb the bitter sarcasm lacing his voice. "Why do you think I'm returning to Volyarus tomorrow? I'll have to play *Head of State* for the month they are gone."

As if his job as CEO of Yurkovich Tanner wasn't enough.

But then his father had fulfilled both roles in the years between his own parents' deaths and when Maks took over as CEO of the company at the age of twenty-five. King Fedir could have hired someone else as CEO for Yurkovich Tanner, as Maks planned to do when he was made official Head of State, but his father insisted on running the company personally.

"Your mother will enjoy your company."

"More than my father's. I know." There was never anything as distasteful as a public row between his parents, but it was also no secret that they were not the best of friends.

His mother lived a completely separate life from his father except when their roles in the monarchy drew them together.

Demyan settled on the corner of Maks's large, antique executive desk. "I think you'll want to put off your flight at least a day."

"Why?" Maks all but growled.

He was looking forward to going back to his homeland and getting out of temptation's way. Nine weeks had not made staying away from Gillian any easier. He wanted her with a hunger he'd never had for another woman. It was inconvenient and frustrating.

Dating other women had only proved to him that when he could still remember driving a brand-new Mercedes sports class, he wasn't going to enjoy getting behind the wheel of a 1980s Volvo station wagon.

He hadn't had sex since his last night with Gillian.

"Ms. Harris made an appointment with a doctor."

Just the sound of her name made that desire in Maks he'd striven so hard to control thump inside him.

Using his formidable control, he evinced little interest in his cousin's words. "So?"

"An obstetrician."

"So, she's looking into fertility treatments." Maks's already dark mood took a turn for the worse. "Making plans for the future."

"Not exactly, no."

"What the hell are you talking about then?"

"According to our hacker, she's confirmed by two blood tests and the baby's heartbeat to be ten weeks' viably pregnant."

"What?" His cousin could not have said what Maks thought he'd heard. "We have a hacker on payroll?"

"Really? That's what you want to know?"

Maks glared at his cousin, his thoughts whirling and no clever retorts springing to mind for the first time in memory.

Demyan grimaced. "Your decision to go without a condom came with consequences."

Maks had never regretted sharing confidences with his older cousin, but he never would have told Demyan about that particular folly if he had not been paralytically drunk, either.

"Impossible!"

"Not so much, no."

"Damn it, Demyan, this is no topic for jokes."

"I am well aware." And Demyan had never looked more serious.

"Are you telling me that Gillian is pregnant with my child?"

"I am telling you that Ms. Harris was given a pregnancy test as part of a checkup for the flu and that test came back positive. A second test was administered. That test also came back positive. A Doppler ultrasound was performed and a baby's healthy heartbeat was recorded. Her file indicates the pregnancy is ten weeks old."

"She has the flu?"

Demyan just looked at him.

Shock had destroyed Maks's usual high level thinking processes. "What?"

"I imagine she went in for the flu and discovered it was morning sickness."

"Oh." Maks hadn't spent much time in the company of pregnant women, but even he knew about morning sickness. He should have realized immediately. "Is she all right?"

"I did not speak to your former girlfriend, Maks. I read a report from our investigative agency."

The reality of what Demyan was telling him, and all that it implied, finally and completely pierced his mind's stupor. Maks swore vehemently and at length in Ukrainian.

Demyan didn't flinch, though he understood the words as well as Maks. "You believe you are the father."

"Of course I'm the father. Gillian doesn't sleep around."

"She could have bedded another man in reaction to you dumping her."

The very thought infuriated Maks, but he kept all expression from his face. Even his cousin wasn't privy to Maks's innermost thoughts.

He didn't hide his displeasure at Demyan's description of the breakup however. "I didn't *dump* her. I was forced to end our relationship for the sake of the Crown."

"Because she could not give you children."

The irony was not lost on Maks. "Yes."

"What are you going to do?"

"What I planned to do before I found out her fallopian tubes are compromised. Marry her." There was no other option.

This child might well be their only child, but it would be *his* and that was a fact Maks would never dismiss.

CHAPTER FOUR

Gillian shut the door behind her grandparents and sagged against it, free to do nothing to hide her fatigue and nausea for the first time in a week.

It had been touch and go for a while there, but Gillian had successfully hidden her pregnancy from the older couple. She had an entire lifetime's experience protecting them from truth that would hurt.

She had spent her childhood doing a very good job of keeping how devastating their beloved son's neglect of his only child had been to her emotions and ability to trust. Gillian had convinced them she did not mind only seeing her mother once a year, and that her father's more frequent but still sporadic and mostly impersonal visits were just fine.

To this day, neither of her grandparents knew how many nights she'd cried silently in her bed at night because neither of her parents would allow her to call them by anything but their first names. No mom or dad, or even mother and father.

Nothing to indicate that Gillian *belonged* to them.

She rubbed her hand over her still flat stomach. The

baby growing in her womb would never doubt its place in her life.

Unfortunately her own poor judgment meant she couldn't guarantee the same from her baby's father.

That knowledge, more than any other, caused her sleepless nights now.

Sighing, she moved into the bedroom. Time to get ready for work. She'd taken the week off to spend with her grandparents, but her boss and clients expected her in the studio later that morning.

Ten hours later, Gillian had put a full day in at the photography studio and stumbled into her apartment well after her usual dinner hour. Dragging with exhaustion, she popped some corn in the microwave for dinner.

Her plans for the evening included watching reruns of *Extreme Makeover—Home Edition* in her pajamas on the couch. She could do with some feel good, full on sap programming right now.

The door buzzer sounded and she had a terrible irrational thought that her grandparents had decided to stay in town for a while, but she dismissed it.

She'd gotten a quick call from Nana when they reached the Canadian border. They wouldn't have turned around without reason and she hadn't given them one.

It could possibly be her father. Rich was known to drop in without warning, but his unexpected visits were as infrequent as the planned ones.

She had friends, but one result of her upbringing and moving to the big city from a small Alaskan town was that she didn't invite many of them to her home. That had only gotten more acute the last year as she'd dated a man who could define circumspect with his social life.

Leaving the popcorn to finish, she crossed to the intercom box and pressed the communication button. "Yes."

"It is me, Gillian. Let me up."

Maks's voice.

Her fist came up to her chest, between her breasts, and she gulped in air. How could such a small thing wreak such devastation?

But his voice had the power to take her to her knees. Literally. It was only leaning onto the wall that kept her upright.

What was he doing here? In ten weeks, he hadn't so much as texted her to see if she was all right.

And now he showed up at her door?

"Gillian?" His voice sounded tinny through the intercom. "Are you there?"

"Yes," she croaked, her mouth and throat dry.

"You haven't pushed the release for the door."

And he was surprised?

She swallowed and took a breath, trying to ease the tightness in her chest. "What are you doing here?"

"We need to talk."

A week, or even two after he'd left, she would have welcomed those words. "It's been three months."

"Not quite. Ten weeks."

So, he'd tracked the time. It didn't mean anything. "What do you want, Maks?"

"Let me up and I will tell you."

"I don't want to see you." She'd just gotten to the point where she could go to sleep without a physical ache to be with him.

And that didn't happen every night.

"I will make it all right."

He didn't love her. Didn't want her. Thought she was defective. How did he make that okay? "No."

"Gillian."

A small voice laced with that horrible emotion hope whispered to her that at least he was here *now*. This was better than her approaching him with news of her pregnancy and facing "duty driven" Maks. Wasn't it?

There was only one way to find out.

It took more courage than she expected for her to give her tacit agreement to see him, but she was not weak.

She also wasn't overjoyed to have Maks seeking access to her apartment. "You'll have to keep it short, I'm tired."

He didn't reply and she didn't expect him to. It wasn't the empty admonishment it might have been before she rang security on him the last time he'd been to her apartment.

Gillian pressed the button to open the downstairs security door before very pointedly returning to the kitchen.

She'd showered after getting home from work and hadn't bothered to do anything but pull her hair into a ponytail and slip into her favorite pajamas since.

For the first time since meeting Maks, Gillian didn't care that she wasn't looking her best to see him. She wasn't about to go rushing around trying to look gorgeous for a man who had ejected her from his life with the efficiency and power of a missile launcher.

She was pouring the popcorn into a bowl when the doorbell rang.

Carrying the bowl, she made her way to the apartment's front door. She only had to take three deep breaths and give herself one very stern reminder she was in control here before opening it.

Maks looked a little less than his immaculate self, too. His almost black hair was messy, like he'd been running his fingers through it. He'd lost his tie between the office and her apartment and he'd skipped his second shave of the day, leaving the five o'clock shadow to darken his cheeks and jaw.

Ten weeks ago, she would have found that incredibly sexy. She also would have taken his state as proof he felt comfortable enough to be himself in her presence.

Now, it worried her a little.

Had their separation been hard on him, too? She had a very hard time believing he was here in hopes of getting back together. As far as he knew, nothing had changed.

She wasn't making any assumptions this time, one way or another, though. Whatever he wanted, whatever he was feeling, he'd have to come out and say it. In words that could not be mistaken to mean something else.

If he was looking for reconciliation, however, she had no idea how she would respond.

Things had changed for her, unequivocally, but one thing hadn't. He didn't love her.

Her stomach roiled with stress and she forced herself to take shallow breaths so she did not retch.

The one saving grace to this situation was that he didn't know she was pregnant. That, at least, wasn't on the table to complicate things further.

He reached out as if to touch her. "You're pale."

"I'm tired." She stepped back, not allowing that casual connection to happen.

It wouldn't be good for her campaign to get over him.

"So you said." He almost seemed lost for words.

"Come inside."

He nodded, the movement jerky, and followed her into the living room. She set the popcorn bowl on the table next to the glass of milk she'd poured herself earlier. "Would you like something to drink?"

He nodded and then shook his head. "You shouldn't be drinking."

"Because I'm tired?" She shrugged. "I'm not going to fall asleep on you. Besides, I'm drinking milk."

"Good. That's great."

She didn't respond. Seeing him was stirring memories and feelings that brought pain and hope, both in debilitating degrees.

The hope scared her the most. A lot of people didn't realize just how truly terrifying hope could be. Particularly for someone whose hopes had been dashed as many times as hers had been.

There was a cost for believing in someone bound to disappoint. Someone like her charismatic, famous and perennially distanced father.

Deciding a more relaxed Maks would be better for both of them, she crossed to her small bar and poured him a whiskey.

He was standing right behind her when she turned to hand it to him, making her jump back.

He reached out to grab her. "Careful!"

"Don't have a conniption." Once again, she jerked out of the path of his potential touch. "I wasn't going to fall and I wouldn't have been startled if you hadn't been hulking behind me. Take your drink and sit down."

He frowned, but then nodded almost meekly and did just that.

Gillian wasn't exactly sure what to do with an awkward, meek Maks. Maybe it was her pregnancy hormones, but she wasn't feeling any big urges to make him more comfortable, either.

She took her own seat, grabbing a handful of popcorn and starting to eat it one kernel at a time. Her stomach needed settling and she wasn't standing on ceremony to do it.

"Is that your dinner?" Maks asked, sounding truly appalled.

"Yes."

"But that is hardly adequate nourishment."

"It's fine."

"But…"

She rolled her eyes. "Did you come here to talk to me about my eating habits or something else? News of our former relationship hasn't leaked to the press, has it?" she asked, the prospect a truly dismaying one.

"No."

"Good."

"Yes, that would complicate matters in ways we do not need at the present."

"What matters? I'm not sure why you're here, Maks."

"Aren't you?"

She wanted to believe it was because the prince couldn't live without her, but somehow Gillian knew that particular fairy tale wasn't for her. "No."

"We have a very delicate situation and if we do not handle it correctly, it will blow up in our faces."

"The delicate situation of…"

"You can drop the pretense. I *know.*"

"You know?" What did he know?

His gaze drifted to her stomach and then back to hers.

The dread of certainty filled her. But there was *no way* he could know she was pregnant. "Either tell me why you're here, or have your drink and leave."

"The baby."

"How?" she demanded as any hope she'd felt got crushed under the reality of truth. Again.

He wasn't here because he missed her too much to stay away. He wasn't here for *her* at all.

"Demyan."

"Demyan what? Bribed my doctor for information? But why would he?" None of this made any sense.

"He assigned typical post-relationship surveillance."

"You had me followed?" she asked, sick at the thought of strangers watching her.

She'd never foreseen this particular complication to dating a prince. Particularly when they'd taken such care to keep their relationship out of the eyes of the media. She'd never even considered *Maks* would be the source of such invasive actions.

She should have, but she'd been blind to a lot about her time with Maks.

"I did not, though I should have. When were you going to tell me? Or did you plan to get revenge by not telling me at all?"

"What a stupid question. At what point during our time together did I *ever* give you the impression I thought it was acceptable to make children pay for the poor choices of their parents?"

The question hung between them like a gauntlet thrown down and Maks knew he had no place picking it up.

She was right. This woman was not motivated by revenge or negative feelings.

The fact she had any sort of a relationship at all as an adult with parents who had shamefully neglected her as a child was testament to the fact Gillian's heart was more forgiving, not to mention tolerant, than most.

"I am sorry. That was uncalled for," he admitted,

though apologizing was not his forte and never had been. "When *were* you going to tell me?"

"Once I had gotten through the first trimester."

"Surely you realize the sooner I knew and appropriate action could be taken, the better."

"Appropriate action?" she asked, her expression completely closed to him for once.

"Marriage." What else could they do?

"I see."

She did not seem in the least excited at the prospect, though he was certain she had wanted nothing more than his proposal ten weeks ago.

Armed with the knowledge that she had *not* realized it was their last night together, he'd had time...much too much time...to go over that last night and the following morning in his head. The conclusions he had drawn were not all pleasant. Nor did they paint him in the best of lights from her perspective.

He comprehended that.

It almost made her action of calling for security that final morning understandable. Not entirely so, but almost. Such precipitous behavior would not be acceptable going forward, however.

No doubt his mother would explain things of that nature to a woman she would groom to take the position of queen one day.

At present, there was enough on the table for discussion without focusing on past behavior.

"You are taking a lot for granted, aren't you?" she

asked before he said anything else, or responded overtly to her noncommittal *I see.*

"My child will be heir to the throne of Volyarus." Surely she understood that.

Gillian's bright blue eyes lit with challenge. "Even a girl?"

"Yes. The monarchy passes to the oldest child of the monarch, male or female does not matter."

"How progressive."

"Not really. Many monarchies have no masculine stipulation for title bequeathal."

"Really? I didn't know." She dropped the popcorn she'd picked up back into the bowl and pushed her milk glass two inches to the right.

Maks admitted, "My father's generation could have stood to be more progressive."

"What do you mean?" Gillian asked.

"The business and political roles have always been shared amidst the siblings of the ruling family. My father was not open to having his sister's help in running Yurkovich Tanner."

"Oh." Clearly Gillian had expected him to say something else.

"His attitude toward provision of an heir is also archaic." His father had married his mother for the sole sake of children, because the woman he loved could not provide them.

They had ended up with a single child and no accord.

"Yes, it is."

Even though he'd voiced the criticism himself, having Gillian agree so quickly pricked at Maks's pride and sense of familial loyalty. However, he refrained from making excuses for his father.

"You look tired." She looked completely exhausted.

"I am."

"What is the matter?"

"Nothing. Apparently it's a normal part of pregnancy."

He did not like that answer at all. He needed information on pregnancy from someone with specialized knowledge. That was clear.

"There is as much as a twenty percent chance this pregnancy will not be viable." She spoke in a monotone, so at first her words did not sink in. "That number goes down to three percent once the baby makes it past twelve weeks."

The imperative to consult with an expert grew astronomically. "What? Why is the risk so high?"

"Apparently miscarriage is a lot more common than you'd expect." The casual tone of her words was belied by the tense line of Gillian's shoulders.

"My child will not miscarry."

Gillian shook her head, her expression mocking. "You don't have much to say about it."

"I do not believe that. There must be something we can do."

"*I'm* doing it. I take a highly soluble prenatal vitamin and folic acid. I've switched my exercise regime to one approved for pregnant women. I've given up caffeine and alcohol, though my doctor says I can indulge in both in small quantities. I do *nothing* to put undue stress on my womb." Determination darkened her blue eyes.

"You want this child." The jury was still very much out on whether or not she wanted *him,* but Maks had no doubts Gillian wanted their child.

"More than you could possibly understand. I plan to be an exemplary mother."

"Your grandmother set a high standard to follow." And Gillian's mother had shown his former lover just exactly what she did not want to be as a parent.

An almost smile curved Gillian's lips and she warmed infinitesimally toward him. "Yes, Nana did."

"She must be excited about the baby." It bothered him that someone else knew about their child before he had.

He recognized the reaction as unreasonable, but that did not diminish his feeling of disappointment.

"I have not told her."

That shocked him. Gillian told her grandmother everything. She'd been willing to keep their dating out of the public eye, but not her family's. He had met her grandparents and gone through a grilling unlike anything he'd experienced before as a Crown Prince.

Neither of the older Harrises had treated him like royalty and he'd actually enjoyed it.

Gillian had even met his own mother on a few social occasions as well.

So, why keep the news of the baby from her grandmother? Because Gillian wasn't married?

"I don't think your grandmother would judge you for getting pregnant before the wedding, Gillian."

"She's more old-fashioned than you realize. Who do you think pushed the issue of my parents marrying to *legitimize* my birth?"

Which might well make her grandmother his best ally. He filed that bit of information away for later use if need be.

"I'm not telling *anyone* about the baby until I've made it past my twelfth week," Gillian offered in explanation.

She was taking the possibility of miscarriage very seriously. "You need to stop thinking in this negative way."

"I'm not thinking negatively. I'm being realistic."

He did not agree. "Realistic is you are pregnant and we must determine how best to react to that truth."

Gillian's general air of tired pessimism morphed into anger faster than he could track.

She glared fiercely. "I'm reacting to it just fine."

For the entire eight months they had dated, he'd been convinced of Gillian's practical nature. However, that final night had shown a romantic streak he should have guessed at from the beginning.

She earned her living predominately doing photography for the covers of romance novels. Gillian was far too good at it not to be at least a closet romantic, no matter how well she tried to hide it.

Maks knew he wasn't the most aware man on the planet when it came to interpersonal relationships, particularly those with women. He was a stellar diplomat and had no superior among his contemporaries in business savvy. However, past liaisons had proven those skills did not extend into the realm of lovers.

None of his former liaisons remained in the "friend" category, something Demyan found highly amusing.

And still, Maks had the unexpected and unquestionable revelation that only one thing would suffice in the present circumstances. It had precipitated making a stop at Tiffany's on the way to Gillian's apartment.

Pulling the pale aqua blue box from his pocket, he dropped to his knee in front of his pajama clad ex-lover. "Will you marry me, Gillian Harris?"

CHAPTER FIVE

She stared at him and then at the ring box like it might snap open at any moment to reveal angry wasps rather than a very expensive engagement ring worthy of not just any princess, but the woman who would bear that title for Volyarus.

"You brought a ring." She sounded dazed by the fact and not at all happy.

"You deserve all the trimmings, but you would not appreciate them after the way our last time together ended." Kneeling before her felt awkward; he was glad it was not a position he would be in again anytime soon.

What was romantic about this?

"You are right. The *trimmings* would be wasted after your *honesty* ten weeks ago."

There was no good response to that, so he didn't make one.

Opening the box, he revealed the large square cut diamond with yellow diamonds to either side of it. Set in platinum, all the stones were of unparalleled clarity. "Marry me, Gillian."

"It's a beautiful ring." She gave it a brief glance and then looked away, as if she could not bear to see it.

He did not understand why. Didn't women like jewelry? His mother certainly did. Though she insisted on nothing ostentatious, she expected significant gifts each year on the anniversary of her marriage to his father.

"You are a beautiful woman."

Her bow-shaped lips twisted in a moue of disagreement. "If I were one of the astonishingly beautiful people, you would not have been interested in me."

It was true. He might have bedded her, but he would not have *dated* Gillian if she was a woman who drew media attention merely from her looks alone. That did not mean, however, that she was not lovely.

"I have never missed a woman after our liaison ended." She deserved the admission, though he didn't like making it.

"You didn't do a lot of dating before me."

It was true, but he had been in two almost-serious relationships. Neither had ended well. Both had reinforced an important truth: love only compromised duty.

"I missed *you*," he reiterated in case she missed the point the first time.

She tucked her body into the corner of the couch, her feet up on the cushions, her arms wrapped around her knees. "Am I supposed to be impressed? You dumped me."

It had been the expedient action, but if he reminded her of that salient fact, he did not think it would do him any favors in the present. "I have since regretted my decision."

"When you found out I am pregnant."

He could not deny it, so he remained silent. Though he had been unhappy about the decision before that, he had not allowed himself to regret it.

She sighed, glanced at the ring and then looked away again. "I'm not committing to anything until I've made it past my first trimester."

"That is not acceptable."

"Nine weeks ago, you made it very clear you did not want to marry me unless I could provide heirs for the throne. If I miscarry, the situation will be the same as before with the identical low chance of me conceiving again." The pain that knowledge caused her bled into her tone, but her expression showed none of it.

He had no way of knowing if that pain came from the knowledge conception was not a given for her, or that *they* would have little future if she could not do so.

Even so, his first instincts were to disagree with her dictate.

He moved to sit beside her on the sofa, acutely aware of the tiny move she made farther into her corner. "Every day we wait to announce our forthcoming marriage is a day in which someone in the press may stumble across your condition and then we'll be the center of a media storm."

"Unless they're also bribing doctors, no one is going to find out about my *condition,* Maks."

"Demyan did not bribe your doctor."

"Then how did he find out?"

"I don't think you really want to know."

"I do."

"A hacker."

"You had my medical records hacked?" she asked in shock-laced anger.

"Demyan—"

"Right, it was your cousin. Not you."

"Nevertheless, we would be foolish to assume no one else could find out. There are doctor's appointments—"

"I don't have another one until my twelve-week mark," she said, interrupting him a second time.

He just looked at her. She knew, maybe even better than him, how easily the press got hold of information people believed locked in the strongest vault.

"You work very hard to stay out of the limelight, don't you?"

"Volyarus is best served by its monarchy maintaining a low profile in the media."

"Why?"

"With the interest of the press comes the interest of the world, an interest that can quickly morph into political agendas and twisted perceptions. Volyarus has thrived as a little-known country with strategic location coupled with significant natural resources."

Some might think that because of the name, Volyarus was a country of Russian descent, but they would be wrong. Very wrong. Volyarus was a shortened version of a Ukrainian saying that meant freedom from Russia.

His antecedent had been a Hetman in Ukraine before Russia overtook the country. Seeing what the future held, he and a group of nobles and laborers had left Ukraine to settle on the island in the Baltic Sea that became Volyarus.

While Ukrainian was only spoken sporadically by the many living in Ukraine today, because of the Russian control for so many years, it was still the official and most prevalent language of Volyarus.

Citizens were required to be proficient in at least one other language before finishing the equivalent of high school in the U.S.A. Maks himself spoke four fluently and three additional languages with enough proficiency to travel without an interpreter.

And yet he found communicating with this woman an incredible challenge.

"Everything in your life is about Volyarus, isn't it?"

"Yes." He would not apologize for that fact, nor would he change it.

He was born to a duty few could comprehend, but a burden he had never resented. His place in the world was immutable, but then he'd never *wanted* to change it.

"Even more reason not to put the country in the limelight with a failed engagement landing on the tail of a miscarriage."

"I would not break our engagement if you miscarried." Though he should. It was the only course of action that made sense.

However, no one could deny the fact she'd gotten pregnant after *one* time making love without a condom.

They were clearly compatible chemically and even

if she were to lose this baby, though he was sure she was not going to, she *would* become pregnant again.

Besides, it wasn't an engagement they'd be breaking, but a marriage. The only politically expedient action in the circumstances was an elopement followed by a reception of extreme pomp.

His mother would be thrilled to plan it. She liked Gillian, had made her approval of the choice clear. She wouldn't be as happy about the timing of the pregnancy, but his mother was not the type of woman to bemoan what could not be changed.

The queen of Volyarus would expect an immediate elopement however.

He didn't bring any of this up, however. There would be time enough to convince Gillian to marry him *immediately* once she agreed to marry him at all.

"You're assuming I'll agree to marry you," she said as if reading his mind.

He dropped the ring in her lap and stood. "What choice do either of us have?"

"Lovely."

He didn't respond to her sarcasm. Perhaps it hadn't been elegantly phrased, but it was the truth.

"Even if I didn't want to marry you, I would." He gave gratitude that he did in fact like the idea of marriage to his lovely blonde.

"Even better."

He swore. He was usually much better at diplomacy, though once again his lack in the interpersonal arena was reaching out to bite him on the ass.

Maks prowled the room, stopping in front of the drinks cabinet. Not about to pour another whiskey when his first one remained practically untouched, he spun away. She could argue all she liked, the fact remained she carried the heir to the Volyarus throne. Gillian *had* to marry him.

"And you wouldn't be considering this course of action otherwise." No bitterness laced her tone. Just flat acceptance.

Still, he knew that fact did *not* make her happy.

He turned to face her. "Does it really matter? The baby you carry is nothing short of a miracle. Our miracle."

"Yes."

"So, you will marry me."

"Yes, the baby is a miracle, but yes, it matters," she clarified, her lovely features set in determined lines. "I'm not making any commitments for another two weeks. You can argue until your throat is raw with it, but I won't be changing my mind on that fact."

There was no give in her tone, no evidence of possible softness in her blue gaze. He was not used to seeing Gillian as the hardline taker, but there could be no question. This woman would *not* be moved.

"Then in two weeks' time we will be married."

"I'm not making any promises—"

"Until you've hit your second trimester. I heard you the first time."

"So, stop trying to push for a promise I'm not prepared to make."

"But you will make it."

"I don't know."

"You do." She must. "You made your choice."

"What do you mean?"

"You knew dating me came with different expectations than other men."

"I didn't sign my life over to you when I agreed to see you exclusively."

They'd never verbalized that agreement, but he took her point.

It just wasn't the salient one. "You did not know about your compromised fallopian tubes when you agreed to make love without a condom."

"We had sex and you made the same choice."

"I believed pregnancy was impossible, or at least extremely unlikely," he felt compelled to add.

"Unlucky you."

"That is *not* how I see it."

She frowned and then enlightenment dawned, but he held no confidence she'd seen light about the right thing. "No, I suppose you think me being pregnant with your child is lucky indeed. The heir is on the way."

"I will treasure our child, and not merely because he or she is the heir to the throne of Volyarus."

"Will you? Really?" she asked intently.

"Yes." There could be no doubt.

"That's something, I suppose."

"My parents were king and queen of a small but still demanding nation. Nevertheless, they were very good parents."

"Even though your father split his time between your family and his *friend* the countess?"

"No one's home life is ideal, but mine was good. Our child's will be better."

"That's what I want for my child. Better. I want her, or him, to know unconditional love."

"Like you did from your grandparents."

"Like I wanted from either or both of my parents."

She'd never voiced that desire before, though he could have guessed at it.

"We are not your parents."

"We aren't yours, either."

It was his turn to ask what she meant.

"If, and I do mean *if,* I agreed to marry you, there would be requirements."

"Like?"

"Like, no mistresses. I'm not your mother and I won't tolerate a long-standing or short-standing affair, or one-night stand for that matter. I would leave you and you'll sign a prenup giving me primary custody in the event of your infidelity."

"I am not my father." Maks was determined *not* to emulate the other man when it came to this area of his father's life. "The king's long-standing understanding with the countess is not something I will ever repeat."

"I'm the only one in your bed. Full stop. Period."

He hated she felt the need to make the stipulation because he knew this was about his father's choices not any Maks had made. He'd never cheated on a lover, even in his college days.

And he never considered his position made him immune to the rules of honor in regard to his future wife, either. "Again, I am not my father."

"You put Volyarus first, last and always."

"But my father does not."

"You don't mean that," she said in obvious shock.

Well, she might be. He didn't criticize his father often and he'd done so twice in one day to her. But if they were to be married, he would not pretend wholesale support of his father's decisions as he did for public consumption.

Like Demyan, Gillian would be privy to things Maks would never express elsewhere. "If my father put Volyarus first and in all ways, he would not continue a liaison that could explode in our faces at any time."

"Your outrage at your father's behavior is based on your concern for Volyarus, not your mother."

"My mother was well aware of the countess when she agreed to marry my father."

"If I am unable to conceive a second time, we will use a surrogate or pursue fertility measures. You will not leave me for a more fertile woman and that would be in any prenuptial between us."

"Fine." Though he didn't know how she planned to ensure that one.

"The prenuptial will include any future offspring in that custody agreement."

"You would have primary custody of any child I conceived with another woman?" He couldn't help the appreciation of her planning lacing his tone.

The woman was not only intelligent, but she knew how to be ruthless. He could appreciate that fact.

"Exactly."

"And if the mother doesn't agree?"

"She'll be forced to fight the Crown in a very messy custody battle right in the center of the media's eye."

"You will use your connections to your father to bring Volyarus into the public eye?"

"You have no idea how far I will go to protect my children's future and their happiness."

"I was raised by a woman willing to sacrifice anything for mine, I do know."

"Oh, no, your mother never fought the way I would fight. She's too wrapped up in the good of Volyarus to push as hard as I would."

That was true. "She is not weak."

He used to think otherwise, but had come to appreciate his mother's brand of strength.

"No, but she is too self-sacrificing. I won't be her."

"You won't be your parents, either. You'll never deny your child its birthright." The way she was talking made him realize just how much time Gillian had spent since discovering she was pregnant thinking about the scenario of a marriage between them.

There could be no doubt the prospect no longer thrilled her, but she clearly understood the importance of protecting their child and his birthright.

"I don't have to marry you for you to name our child as your heir."

"According to Volyarussian law, I can name any living relative as my successor, but the birth of a legitimate heir negates all previous claims to the throne."

"You're saying if you marry someone else and they have a child, that child inherits the throne?" she asked carefully and with clear thought.

"Exactly."

"Fine."

Shock coursed through him. "You would deny our child his place in life?"

In no scenario had Maks expected categorical denial.

"I'm not saying what I would do. You do not seem to be getting that. I'm acknowledging the consequences if I choose not to marry you."

"You cannot do that to our child!" She must realize that.

"You walked out on me ten weeks ago."

"And our child must pay because of it?"

"I have to make the best choice for this baby, one way or another. He or she deserves the best I can give. That may, or may not be, marriage to you."

"Damn it. Why?"

"You don't love me." She put her hand up when he made as if to speak. "In your mind, that doesn't matter. I know, but it matters to me and I have to decide if I can be the best mother possible married to a man who does not love me and who found it so easy to discard me."

"It was not easy."

He could see by the expression on her face that she considered his claim very much a situation of far too little, far too late.

And her words proved it. "It was easy enough. You wouldn't be here if you hadn't found out by nefarious means that I am pregnant."

"It was hardly nefarious means."

"You managed to get information in my confidential medical records. What would you call it?"

"Expedient."

She laughed, the sound both unexpected and welcome. "You're a piece of work, Maks, you know that?"

"I am a prince."

"Who thinks he has the right to put surveillance on an ex-girlfriend."

"I told you—"

"Demyan did it. I knew you two were like brothers. I didn't know that extended to finger pointing."

"He was doing what he thought best."

"Why? I wasn't going to go to the tabloids. You had to realize that."

"I told him about that night."

"What?"

"That we did not use condoms."

"Oh. You told him? Really?"

"Yes, really."

"Why?" She clearly could not see him sharing confidences.

"I was drunk."

"Oh." Her brows furrowed. "Why?"

"I missed you." Hadn't they already been over this?

"You said."

"I meant it."

"I guess you did."

"What? You thought I was lying."

"If it meant convincing me to your point of view? Yes."

"You do not trust me at all." That shocked him.

He was eminently trustworthy.

"No, I don't."

"That is not acceptable."

"You say that a lot. You can't deny that it took finding out I was pregnant to bring you back here. What is there to trust in that?"

"You know why."

"I know I didn't rate even considering fertility treatments."

He had no answer for that. The truth was not always palatable.

"You never doubted the baby is yours?" she asked.

"No."

"Oh, right…you had me followed. You would have known I didn't so something crazy like sleep with a stranger to make myself feel better."

She sounded like that might have been in the offing and he did not like knowing that at all. "It never even crossed my mind you would have sex with another man."

"We weren't together. Why not?"

"You don't sleep around."

"People do crazy things when they're hurting."

He shrugged. He wouldn't know. Self-control had been drilled into him from the cradle. "You didn't."

"No, I didn't."

"Do not sound so miffed by that fact. I am very pleased about it."

"Did you?"

"Did I what?" And then he understood what she wanted. "No other women."

"Why?"

"I missed you." It didn't sound so naff now that he was trying to get her back with interest.

"I might just believe you."

CHAPTER SIX

GILLIAN FELT AS if the universe was conspiring with the Prince of Volyarus to keep him uppermost in her thoughts every second of every day.

As if it wasn't hard enough to get him out of her head as it was.

While photography for book covers comprised the majority of her work, it did not dominate it completely. Usually.

For three days running, every single shoot Gillian had done was for a *romance* cover. *Every single one.* And why all of the heroines were blonde she didn't know.

She often photographed brunette heroines, redheads, even one who had pinks streaks in her hair, but not for the past three days. All her female models were decidedly of the light haired variety.

And they'd all been paired with tall, handsome, dark haired love interests.

None of the men were a patch on Maks, though. They lacked the underlying steel in his character, that cold aloofness that had allowed him to walk away from her without a backward glance.

These models might be amazing men in their own right, but none were Maks. None made Gillian's heart stutter, her breath catch, or her body heat.

And their very differences made Maks even harder to forget.

He wasn't helping, either, not giving her a moment to collect her scattered thoughts.

Maks texted her several times a day. The bits of info on pregnancy were understandable, even charming. His short messages were geared as much toward her comfort as they were the baby's health. She appreciated him not making her feel like a brood mare.

But he acted as if they were still dating, wanting to go to dinner, take her to a show, asking if she was available to be his plus one at upcoming social events.

As if on cue, her phone announced in a snooty tone, "Your text has been served, madam."

The current pair of models both looked up from where they were getting into position for the first set of shots.

"Do you need to get that?" the dark haired not-Maks asked.

She shook her head. "It will keep."

"Don't worry on our account. Go ahead and check it," the blonde offered with a smile that encompassed both Gillian and the male model.

Oh. The woman was interested. The male cover

model wasn't married and Gillian had no intention of standing in the way of possible romance.

"Thanks." She grabbed the phone and clicked through to the text messages.

La Bayadére is playing. Do you want 2 go?

The fiend. He knew she loved the ballet!

She texted back. Too busy.

She wasn't getting sucked back in. Not until she knew what *she* wanted for the future.

R u sure? Great seats.

The temptation was strong, but she held out. Absolutely sure.

Silence. No reply text, no virtual butler giving her a little smile with his snooty tone.

Feeling unaccountably let down, she called the two models back to work.

Now her thoughts kept going back to the choice ahead of her. A choice that impacted the unborn child in her womb irrevocably.

Gillian would give thanks every single day of her life for her grandparents and their love, but they'd resisted her ever considering them full-on parents.

Maybe at first, they'd hoped her dad would take a more active role in her life. Later, it had been their way of maintaining the illusion that Rich Harris *was* her dad,

when he'd never been more than a financially gener-
ous sperm donor.

He said so himself, laughing about it as if holding
no particular affection for his only child was something
funny rather than tragic.

That was not a destiny she was willing to write into
the stardust of heaven for her own child.

Maks wasn't like Rich, though. The prince loved his
own family, even if the words never passed his lips. It
was in everything he did for them, the way he put the
very select few ahead of his own wants and desires.

His parents. Demyan. They were all afforded the
protection of Maks's considerable will and strength.

It was one of the first things she noticed about him;
his commitment to family had given her false hope for
their own relationship.

He didn't love *her,* but Maks would adore any child
of his and that was a circumstance Gillian simply could
not ignore.

Maks knocked on Gillian's door. He'd been texting and
calling her since leaving her apartment—against his
better judgment—the other night.

She replied to most of his texts and took some of his
calls, though she never returned the ones she didn't.
She'd put off seeing him on one pretext or another, even
refusing his offer of *La Bayadére.*

It was very different than the way she'd behaved
before, when her eagerness for his company had often
caused him to smile on days otherwise very challenging.

He'd never expected Gillian to dig her heels in like she had. This streak of stubbornness was something he had to file away for future reference.

The woman could be supremely intransigent.

He was not used to being treated this way by women, and this woman particularly. He did not like it. He'd had enough.

He had to fly out to Volyarus in the early hours to-morrow and he wasn't leaving Seattle without settling some things between them.

The door flew open to reveal Gillian glaring at him in bad temper. "How did you get into my building?"

He shrugged. The hacker had upset her. Telling her he had sublet an apartment on the floor below hers he had never stepped inside so he would have open access to her building would not make her happy, either.

"You are too much."

"I am just enough."

She shook her head and turned toward the kitchen. "You may as well come in. The dinner you had deliv-ered is clearly enough for two. I assume you intend to share it."

"You don't like it?" he asked.

"It's my favorite chicken Parmesan. From a restau-rant that does not do takeout no less, though apparently they do for you. What's not to like?"

He didn't know. So, he said nothing. He'd read preg-nant women could be emotionally unpredictable.

"I appreciate you sending me dinner the last few

nights." The words were grudging, her lovely face set in lines of annoyance rather than gratitude.

Her grandmother would be proud Gillian had remembered her manners when she so clearly would rather tell him to take a flying leap.

"You do not need to be cooking. It's clear you are tired." Too tired to be working full-time, he thought, but was smart enough not to say.

Right then. And though she hadn't allowed him to see her, he had done his best to care for her needs regardless.

"Pregnant women have been cooking their own dinners for millennia."

"This pregnant one does not have to." He laid his hand on her shoulder.

She jolted, like he'd touched her with live electricity, and stepped away from him with an alacrity that troubled him.

"You can no longer bear my touch?" He'd read that some pregnant women went right off sex, too.

He'd hoped Gillian would fall in the other category. The one where pregnancy drove their hormones in quite a different direction. The physicality between them had been something he'd missed sorely over the past months. And he'd hoped to use it to reestablish intimacy between them.

Gillian didn't answer him, but moved to where takeout containers sat open on the counter. With quick, economic movements, she plated the food in silence.

He took glassware and cutlery through to the small dining room.

"I'd prefer to eat on the sofa," she called from the kitchen, sounding every bit as cranky as she'd looked answering the door, not to mention as if she thought he should have known that already.

Not sure how she had expected him to read her mind, he made a quick change of direction, putting the glasses and cutlery down on the coffee table before returning to the kitchen. "What do you want to drink?"

"Milk." Her mouth turned down in obvious dissatisfaction. "It's good for the baby."

"There are many other calcium-rich foods you can eat. You don't have to drink milk if you'd prefer something else."

She used to like milk. Was this one of those pregnancy things?

She glowered at him. "Stop being so nice!"

"You would prefer I was dismissive of your desires?"

"Yes. It would make it easier."

"What?"

"You know what."

"This supposed choice you must make?"

"It's not supposed."

Annoyance rose to match hers, but he controlled it, allowing nothing but certainty to color his tone. "There *is* no choice when it comes to our child, Gillian. You know that, though you refuse to acknowledge it."

"Did your mother have a choice?"

What an odd question to ask, as if Gillian couldn't

imagine his mother marrying his father under any other circumstances. It pricked at Maks's pride.

Perhaps a little of his irritation came through when he said, "She was not pregnant when they married if that is what you mean. In fact, I did not arrive until two weeks after their first anniversary."

"Then *why* did she marry your father?"

Gillian made it sound as if marrying into his family was a fate worse than death. Forget small pricks at his pride, this was a fully realized blow.

"Many women would have been happy to receive my father's marital-minded intentions," he ground out.

Gillian's brow furrowed. "But she knew about the countess when she married him?"

Maks frowned at the mention of his father's *love* affair. Even though they'd discussed it before, he didn't like dwelling on something that had been a source of unpleasantness for his family his entire life. "Yes. Why?"

"I cannot imagine marrying a man who was in love with another woman."

"That is not something you have to worry about." Maks would never allow that particular emotion sway in his heart or his life.

Romantic love only caused pain and undermined duty and dedication.

"You could fall in love with someone else later." Gillian's tone wasn't at all certain.

Good. Even she realized how unlikely that was.

"If I were going to love anyone, I assure you, it would be you." Surely she realized this?

But then what Maks thought Gillian should know and what she actually accepted as truth were widely divergent, he'd come to appreciate.

She shook her head. "Do you have any idea how that sounds, what that does to my heart to hear?"

In truth, clearly he did not. He thought she would have liked knowing that. "You would prefer I withhold the truth?"

"I would prefer you loved me."

He wanted to turn away from the pain in her eyes, but he was not a weak man to refuse to face the consequences of his choices. "I am sorry."

"You said that before you left my apartment ten weeks ago."

"I meant it." He was not a monster.

She frowned and turned back to the plates, sprinkling the fresh Parmesan over the chicken instead of looking at him. "We're going to make a scandal, one way or another."

"Maybe a small one, but nothing truly damaging to the country if we take a proactive approach. My PR team is very good." It would cause some media furor.

His marriage couldn't help but do otherwise, but his PR team would make sure that furor died down quickly and remained mostly positive.

They wouldn't be able to do that if word of the breakup had gotten out before word of the baby and elopement, though.

"Is Demyan on it?"

He didn't understand the question. "You know he's Director of Operations for Yurkovich Tanner."

"I was being facetious. He's just Machiavellian enough to make a really good PR man."

"I'll tell him you said so."

"Do. And tell him it's not nice to hire hackers to break into confidential medical files."

"I will leave that admonishment to you." For his part, Maks was very grateful to his cousin's foresight.

"Don't think I won't say it to him. He might scare everyone in your company, but he doesn't scare me."

"He intimidates."

People said the same about Maks even though he'd played diplomat from the cradle, but Demyan had an edge to him unsmoothed by political expedience.

"He's a scary guy."

"But not to you." They'd had this conversation once before.

She'd finished it by reminding him that she had Maks's protection and that was all she needed to feel safe, no matter how intimidating a guy his cousin was.

The way Gillian's blue eyes flared now said she remembered that conversation, too. But she was clearly not going there with the conversational thread again.

Her lips set in a firm line and she picked up the plates to carry through to the living room.

He shook his head and approached the fridge. He found milk and cherry limeade. He took the juice with him to the living room.

She looked at the carton in his hand and though she tried to frown, he could see she was pleased.

"Your favorite."

"I've been craving it even more lately."

"Your body no doubt wants Vitamin A and C."

"Yes, Dr. Maks."

"I read that pregnancy cravings are often linked to things your body needs for the baby, or because the baby has depleted your stores already."

"I read that, too."

"So, you've been reading up on pregnancy?" She wasn't denying it just because she was cautiously approaching her second trimester. Good.

"Yes."

"According to my research, your chances of miscarriage are closer to ten percent than twenty." Though not all statistics agreed.

Many doctors still considered her chance of miscarriage at or above twenty percent until she hit the twelve-week mark.

It was the added stress she had to be under, pregnant to a man who was not only not yet her husband, but who would one day be king. Those added pressures and the tension between them increased her chances to miscarry.

He did not like it, but the stress of his position could not be avoided. And he did not see how to fix the other if she would not even entertain the idea of marriage until she'd reached that magical time marker in her head.

She looked at him curiously. "You think one in ten is good odds?"

"I do."

She sat down, but didn't argue. For which he was grateful. He didn't want her thinking negatively.

Thought was a powerful weapon.

They'd been eating for a few silent minutes when she turned to him. "Thank you for dinner. It's very good."

He didn't remind her she'd already thanked him. It was an overture.

He took it. "It is. There is no need to thank me. Your care is my responsibility. Thank you for allowing me to stay."

"We aren't together, Maks."

"The baby growing in your womb says otherwise."

"You're so stubborn."

"Have you looked in a mirror lately?"

He surprised her into a giggle and that made Maks smile.

"Nana always said I was sneaky that way. Everyone thinks I'm easygoing because I don't fight what doesn't matter to me."

He began to better understand this woman he had dated for months without realizing once she could be a rock when it came to doing things her own way. "However, what does matter to you, you fight to the last?"

"Something like that."

She hadn't fought for him, or *them* when he said they

had to end things. Despite her words of love Gillian had given in without a single volley to his side.

He felt pain in the center of his chest. Odd. This restaurant didn't usually cause heartburn.

CHAPTER SEVEN

"I HAVE BEEN thinking a wedding onboard a luxury cruise liner. A friend of mine owns a fleet that sails the inside passage to Alaska on one of its routes. Ariston will make certain word of our marriage does not leak out until after the event."

Gillian jumped, startled by Maks's comment. He'd been mostly silent since they began eating dinner.

"I thought you were mulling over business." She laughed more at herself than the situation. "I should have known better. You have a one-track mind."

A single-minded determination that had led him back to her.

Maybe Gillian would have gotten over Maks, eventually. She'd certainly been doing her best to master the unrequited love that tore at her decimated heart every day he'd been gone.

But one short visit had set her back to the beginning, her heart hurting so much it was almost numb with it.

She knew that at some point that numbness would have become a protective blanket over her emotions. Just like it had done sometime in her childhood.

Maks made it clear he wasn't going to let that happen.

"I assure you, my mind is capable of traveling multiple tracks at once."

"I used to think so."

"What has changed your mind?"

"It's either the baby, my pregnancy, or our upcoming marriage—which is not a done deal, no matter what you tell yourself—since you showed up here three days ago."

He settled back into the sofa, one long arm along its back, his left ankle crossed negligently over his right knee. "Those are three tracks."

"Ha, ha."

"I am not attempting humor, merely pointing out a fact. I have also in the last three days negotiated mineral rights for Yurkovich Tanner to a new rare minerals mine in Zimbabwe, overhauled and signed numerous contracts, avoided a political *situation* between Volyarus and Canada if you can believe it, interviewed several candidates for the position of Director of the Ministry for Education in Volyarus, mediated a labor dispute via teleconference in one of our currently operating mines, and finalized a new employee benefits package for the United States employees of Yurkovich Tanner."

Okay. So the man was a machine of efficiency in both the business and political realm. "And still, you've had time to text me several times a day and call me nearly as often."

"That should tell you where you sit in my priorities."

She opened her mouth to say something smart, but

closed it again without speaking. It was true. Maks had made time for her in a schedule that would defeat most men.

He always had.

"You don't love me." It wasn't an accusation, more a statement of confusion.

Why make her such a priority when his interest in her was more for the Crown's sake than his own emotions? But that was her answer, wasn't it?

No effort was too great on behalf of his country and its people. Including finding a wife and mother to the next royal generation.

"I do not believe in love as the all positive, powerful force everyone seems to think it is."

"How would you know?" He wasn't in love.

He'd shattered her scarred heart when he rejected her and let Gillian know in unequivocal terms that he did not love her.

Could she make that important in the face of her child's future, though?

That was the real question. How important was her pain in the balance of things? Both her parents had weighed their feelings, their desires, their careers, even their mildest convenience against their only child's happiness. Gillian had always lost.

She wasn't ever going to do that to her baby.

Maks lifted one dark brow in an unmistakably sardonic gesture challenging her question without words.

And then it clicked. She was being naive, not to mention somewhat myopic, wasn't she? He'd certainly experienced the negative side of love through his father's long-standing affair with the *love of his life.*

"Your father's love for the countess is not the problem, it's what he chose to do with that love."

"So you say."

"He had choices and he opted for the route most thinking people abandoned sometime in the Victorian era."

"Really? You are so sure about that?"

"No, but if the countess was like me, compromised in her reproductive abilities, he still could have married her. They could have used a surrogate."

"And risk having a woman make claims to the Volyarussian throne via her offspring? I do not think so."

"Baloney. There had to be a woman among your countrymen that he could have trusted to sacrifice for the good of the throne in this way."

"He approached my mother. Her dedication to Volyarus was a well-known circumstance."

"And she demanded marriage."

"She believed she would be a better queen than Countess Walek, a divorcée already with no children by her previous marriage."

Gillian couldn't help wondering if Queen Oxana had been in love with King Fedir back then, if her reason for demanding marriage had as much to do with affairs of the heart as the affairs of state.

Maybe like Leah in the Bible, she'd thought if she gave children to her husband she would earn his devotion. It hadn't worked that way for Leah and certainly hadn't for Queen Oxana.

"Your family is all kinds of dysfunctional, isn't it?"

"No more so than yours."

"Touché."

Maks's dark eyes studied Gillian with an expression she couldn't put a name to. "You said you *do* love me."

If she thought he was rubbing it in, she would dump the remainder of the pasta sauce pooled on her plate over his head. His tone was more clinical than gloating however, his expression still that enigmatic mask, but tinged with curiosity she could see.

"So?"

"Yet you did not fight for me."

"What? I fought for you."

"You evicted me from your apartment with haste."

She stared at him. "What did you expect? You'd just dumped me. I wasn't even worth looking into fertility treatments for."

"You could have argued, insisted on doing exactly that. If you wanted to be with me."

Like his mother had fought to be with his father? That had worked out well, hadn't it?

Shoving aside the sarcasm, she still couldn't believe he was trying to put it back on her.

Or was he? In his mind, he was only explaining his stance that love was not a positive, powerful force. And from his perspective, she had to think maybe she could understand why he'd come to that conclusion.

She tried to explain. "You admitted you don't love me."

"I never claimed to love you, but it had to be obvious I was considering marriage to you."

"It was." That was one of the reasons his rejection had hurt so much.

It had been such a shock in the face of what she'd thought were well-placed hopes. Hopes that had confounded her ten weeks ago and now, she still found inexplicable. "Why me? I'm not royal. I'm not anything special."

"That is not true. You are a woman of definite integrity."

"So are women a lot more politically connected than me."

"You have your own connections."

"You dated me because my father is a famous news correspondent?" It wouldn't be the first time, but it would be the first time finding out could hurt enough to make breathing difficult.

"No. I dated you because I was attracted to you. Full stop." His tone left no room for question. "Listen, Gillian, whatever you think of me, I did not want a marriage like my parents. I wanted to tie my life to a woman who would be my complement in every way. You handle yourself in diplomatic circles with an enviable aplomb."

"It's my shyness. I learned to use it to my advantage."

"You come off as reserved but kind. It's exactly what a monarchy like ours needs in its diplomats."

"I'm hardly a diplomat."

"But as princess of Volyarus, you would be."

"It's my mother's connections you find most appealing." That had never happened to her.

"She's a popular politician both in her own country of South Africa and on the international scene."

"Yes, she is." A stalwart feminist, Annalea Pitsu *would* not approve of Gillian marrying into a monarchy and taking a supporting role however. "She is not exactly political royalty, though."

Annalea was a mover and a shaker. Her disappointment with Gillian's choice of career was made clear at each annual visit.

Maks shrugged. "Marrying a woman from another monarchy, particularly a political one, comes with its own set of burdens. None of which have I ever wanted to negotiate."

"But…I don't know…wouldn't your people be happier if you married a Volyarussian?"

"If I had been drawn to a woman from my country as I was drawn to you, I would have pursued her."

"Oh." That told her.

In this, at least, Maks had no intention of being swayed by what the people of his country might prefer. Not the nobility, not the middle class.

There was no poverty class in Volyarus. It was too small and too well run for it.

Maks looked almost nonplussed. "That is all you have to say?"

"You've made it pretty clear you were sexually attracted to me." Not that she was some kind of vamp, or anything.

"I was also attracted to your personality, to the quirky way your mind works, and we have many interests in common."

"You thought I was your ideal woman."

"Yes."

"And then you found out I shouldn't have been able to conceive."

"Not easily, no."

"Were you upset?"

"You could not tell?"

"I thought…" She'd been very careful *not* to dwell on their last night together, but now, looking back, she realized he'd shown a near desperation for what he knew would be their last time together.

Looking at that night in light of what came later, she could see that he had indeed been really upset about breaking up with her.

She almost apologized, before she remembered the choice to walk away had been his. "You made the decision."

He nodded. "And you chose not to fight."

"That's ridiculous," she continued to argue.

What had there been to fight? By his own admission, he hadn't loved her.

What she had to decide now was: would their child be happy in a home where only one parent loved the other one?

Her gut told her, "Yes." In big, lead-heavy letters.

There was no particular pleasure in the knowledge, but there was a certain amount of relief. She could write her child's destiny with a very different brush than her parents had used on Gillian's.

If she had the courage.

If she trusted Maks to let her into that inner circle of his protection, even if he didn't love her.

"You knew I was considering making you the next queen of Volyarus."

"I didn't think of it in those terms, but yes."

"I *did* and you had to know that. Had to know that I was predisposed toward marriage to you, but still you let me go without any effort to convince me to stay."

She couldn't argue that particular point. From his perspective, he was right. "I didn't see any advantage in doing so."

"Did you not? Though you claim to love me."

Maybe she would have been able to convince him. Probably actually. From the way he was talking. That might have made Maks feel weak and even to question his own honor and dedication to duty.

Love ebbed and flowed in life, but Maks's sense of duty never would. If he felt it to her via their children, then it would never wane.

Would it be enough?

The one secret wish she'd cherished in her heart for her entire life was to be so special to just *one* person that they claimed her as irrevocably *theirs* and loved her more than their own convenience.

She'd never expected to come above everything in another person's life. Her aspirations had not been that lofty. And it was a good thing. Even if Maks loved her, he would never put her, or anyone, ahead of his duty to country.

But she'd wanted to be more. More than just the woman who got accidentally pregnant with his heir. More than the woman he could walk away from because her ovaries were flawed.

And if she could not be more, could she be happy?

Looking deep into her own heart, she thought maybe she could.

She stared at him, her heart squeezing in her chest.

No matter her arguments, she knew one thing was true, even if he didn't believe it. "Love is a very powerful force and I do love you."

"Even now?"

"Even now." Had all of this been to get her to admit it?

No. Again, the total lack of triumph on Maks's handsome features spoke for itself.

His strong jaw set in a frown, definitely no victory there. "And you are refusing to even consider marriage to me until you have hit your second trimester. Where is the *great* power of *love* in that?"

Once again, Gillian found herself opening and closing her mouth without the tiniest sound emerging.

He did look smug now, though it was tempered by something she wasn't sure she could name. If she wasn't so certain it was impossible, she'd almost call it vulnerability.

"Unrequited love hurts," she gritted out.

Didn't he realize that?

Sitting up, his agitation evident, he demanded, "In what way am I hurting you?"

"You don't want to be with me."

"I assure you, I do."

"Because of the baby."

"I wanted to ask you to marry me before I knew you were pregnant."

"But my supposed infertility stopped you."

"It is not supposed. It is a medical fact."

"Which means I may never be able to conceive again." He needed to acknowledge that fact and deal with it.

"Then we use a surrogate, or adopt."

"What about the potential problems with the surrogate or adoptive mother?"

"I do not share my father's fears, nor would I be open to my mother's type of ultimatum should my representative approach a likely candidate. I will already be married."

"With an airtight prenuptial agreement."

"Exactly."

She almost laughed, but shock was making her too breathless for that. He *wanted* the prenup. The cagey politician.

"You definitely want more than one child?" she asked.

His parents had stopped after him.

"Yes." Rock solid certainty in that single word.

"Even if it means using a surrogate, or adopting?"

"Yes."

"What about in vitro?" Her hand automatically went to her stomach as she thought of giving the child in her womb a brother or a sister.

"It depends how open you are to multiple attempts at the procedure. We will not risk your health by multiple births of more than twins."

That's what bothered him about in vitro? The risks to her health? "How many children do you want?"

"At least two, but I would like a house full."

She'd been raised an only child, but the mental image of her and Maks surrounded by a brood of children was incredibly appealing. "You live in a castle. That's a lot of children."

He laughed, tension leaving his body as he relaxed again in that wholly appealing pose she tried her best to ignore. "No more than four then."

"Four?" she asked faintly, her heart racing with emotions she didn't want to name.

"We will have help."

"I won't leave the raising of my children to strangers."

"Naturally not, but you will not be required to change every diaper."

She pulled a throw pillow into her lap, resting her arms on it as she tucked her legs up onto the couch. "And you won't change any, being a prince and all."

"I did not say that."

She shook her head. "Right."

"We have strayed from topic."

"What topic is that?"

"You claim loving me hurts you and therefore you cannot commit to marriage to me." Tension seeped subtly back into his frame with each word he uttered.

He did not like the concept at all, she could see that now.

But she wasn't going to lie to him to spare his feelings. He hadn't with hers. "You don't love me."

"So?"

"You aren't making this easy."

"I disagree."

She snorted. "Big surprise."

"You get sarcastic when you are tired, I have noticed."

"I'm not tired." But then she yawned, giving lie to her claim.

He smiled, the expression indulgent. "No, not tired at all."

"Okay, so maybe I am. What's your excuse?" It was getting harder and harder to maintain any level of annoyance with him, so her question came out more teasing than accusatory.

"For?"

"Your sarcasm."

"I'm a sardonic guy."

On that, at least, they could agree.

"You are saying that the mere fact that I do not love you causes you pain?" he asked.

Finally. He got it. "Yes."

"That makes no sense."

"You discarded me so easily because you don't love

me. If you had, you would not have let me go without a thought."

"Like you did me?" he asked, his brow raised in inquiry.

Or simple superiority.

She chose to believe it was the former, but in her heart of hearts she couldn't deny there was some truth to his comparison.

It ignored parts of reality she couldn't, though. "It wasn't without thought. I've missed you terribly."

Another admission she hadn't wanted to make, but had been compelled to because of his willful refusal to understand. Gillian glared at the culprit.

Maks did not appear fazed in the least by her small show of anger. "I missed you as well. I have said so."

"It was your idea to break up," she reminded him with some desperation as she felt the inexorable conclusion of this discussion growing closer and closer.

"I did not feel I had a choice."

Which was exactly why they had to wait to make plans for the future. Plans, she acknowledged, if only to herself, that would include marriage and the title princess in her future. "If I miscarry—"

"Stop talking like that immediately. You are not going to lose this child." His scowl seemed a lot more sincere than her glare had felt.

She didn't want to argue that particular point anyway. And every day closer to her twelve-week mark decreased her chances of losing the baby she'd already grown to love and felt such a fierce protectiveness toward.

"You might fall in love with someone else." She voiced her deepest fear, the one thing that no clause in a prenuptial agreement, no matter how carefully worded, could truly guard against.

No matter what he thought, love was an unstoppable force. He only had to look at his own father. There could be no doubt that Maks had come by his sense of duty and love of country naturally. And yet, the king had maintained a relationship for most of his adulthood that was not good for the Crown.

Because he loved the countess.

Maks looked supremely unconvinced. "That won't happen."

"Even you can't prevent it by sheer force of will."

"Of course I can. It is not merely a matter of will, but of actions. I can guarantee against it without doubt."

She did not share his confidence. "How?"

"Not allowing another woman close enough for a relationship to grow into intimacy that could lead to love, for a start," he said, like it should be obvious.

He had a lot of experience keeping people at bay, but proximity could undermine good intentions. "What if she works for you?"

"This is hypothetical as you well know. My personal office staff are all male, but if I thought a woman who worked for me was attracted to me, I would transfer her, or fire her, depending on how she revealed that attraction."

"You wouldn't be tempted?" Gillian had been to his company's headquarters.

And while his personal office staff might be male, there were still plenty of beautiful women working for Yurkovich Tanner, both in the U.S.A. and in Volyarus.

"No. *Would you?*"

"By another man? Of course not."

"But people in love cheat on each other all the time."

"Not all the time." But it did happen. "Most don't."

"Most? You are sure about that?"

What was she, Dr. Ruth? How should Gillian know? "Nana and Papa never have."

Maks nodded, conceding easily. "They are exemplary people, but they've also protected their marriage vows."

"Yes."

"As will I."

"You're so sure you can't fall in love with someone else."

"You're so sure I can?"

"No, but it's possible." Though the more they talked, the less likely she found it.

This man was determined *never* to be weakened by love. She couldn't believe she'd just realized that about him because, really? It should have been obvious from Day One.

She'd blinded herself to his disdain for the emotion, but it rang through clear when the subject of his father's "vacations" came up.

"And people *in love,* they never fall out of love and fall in love with someone else?" he pushed.

"You know it happens."

"Because they did not protect that love, nurture it, make it paramount."

"You sound like you understand love awfully well for a man who denies its reality."

"Oh, I admit love exists. I deny its all-strengthening positive power. Love undermines duty and makes strong men weak." That he believed every word he was saying could not be denied. It was in every line of his body, his tone and even the determination glowing in his brown eyes. "Insert relationship for love and you have my perspective on our marriage."

She swallowed, struck to the very core with his definition of how to handle marriage. "Our marriage would be that important to you?"

"It would come second to nothing."

He was delusional if he thought that. "That's not true."

"You accuse me of lying."

"About this? Definitely. Volyarus comes first, last and always with you. Our marriage won't trump that— it wouldn't even if you loved me."

"But our marriage is of paramount importance to our country's well-being. Stability in the monarchy has always marked stability for Volyarus."

They weren't talking about the same thing. "If it came between an important political event and our anniversary, the event would win."

"I am a better planner than that."

"Some things are unavoidable."

"Fewer than you might imagine."

Was he making a promise? The expression in his dark eyes said he was.

Against her better judgment, Gillian wanted to believe him. Her unique upbringing had taught her that even if a person didn't give the right name to it, they could have a necessary role in her life.

Like her grandparents, true mom and dad though they would never stand for being called that.

They had given her so much throughout her life, putting off their own dreams of early retirement and travel to see her raised.

Maks was offering her the same kind of commitment. It didn't come wrapped in the pretty bow of love, but it wasn't something to simply dismiss as unworthy, either.

No, Maks committed to her wasn't something to dismiss lightly at all.

"Why a cruise ship?" she couldn't help asking.

Now triumph flared in his espresso gaze. "Ariston can guarantee word of the wedding does not get out before we want it to."

"Ariston?"

"Spiridakous."

"The shipping magnate?" She wasn't in the least surprised Maks was friends with someone so wealthy and powerful.

The man would be king one day and was already

CEO of a company hugely competitive in the global market even though few people even realized it existed.

"His company is solidly diversified."

"With a cruise line?" It must be nice.

"Among other things."

"You only brought up the inside passage cruise because you know it's one I've wanted to go on." She'd mentioned it once.

Just *once,* but this man never forgot *anything* she was coming to realize.

"I will always try to meet your desires."

CHAPTER EIGHT

"Always?" she asked, feeling a sense of inevitability wash over her quickly followed by that irrepressible emotion: hope.

If she was burned by it again, she wasn't sure her heart would survive it. "We should wait until after the baby is born. To be sure."

"No. Stop. I have told you. No more of this negative thinking."

"I'm just trying to be realistic."

He laughed. Like she'd said something incredibly funny. "You are one of the worst pessimists I have ever known."

"I am not. I'm an optimist."

"In Eeyore's universe, maybe."

"You like Winnie the Pooh?"

"My mother read the books to me as a child, just like your grandmother did you. I was not raised on a different planet."

"No, I know. I just…" She wasn't sure what she wanted to say.

Telling him she didn't think he'd had anything that

normal in his childhood wouldn't go over well. And it wouldn't be true, either.

"If you are an optimist, then you will believe in our future and that of our child."

"Wow. You're so sure of yourself."

"I am not wrong."

"You are arrogant."

"Sometimes."

A lot more often than that, but saying so would just be querulous. And she didn't *want* to be argumentative. Not right now. She wanted to dive into his arms and have him tell her everything would be okay.

But she'd left those kinds of fairy tales in childhood.

The thought of approaching him for physical comfort sparked a strange sort of tension inside her as well.

Wanting a minute to regroup (as she was dangerously close to giving in), she stood and picked up the plates. "I'll just put these in the kitchen."

"Let me help." He jumped to his feet, quickly gathering the other detritus of their casual meal.

"I'm pregnant, not helpless."

"You didn't see me taking the plates right out of your hand, did you?" His smile was teasing, his expression unexpectedly lighthearted.

"No," she admitted grudgingly.

"There you have it. *Polite,* not overly protective."

Not entirely sure she minded overly protective or that he'd avoided it altogether, she found herself smiling back.

They fell into a surprisingly easy and natural rhythm

as the dishes were rinsed and put in the dishwasher. "You're awfully domesticated for a prince."

"So you've said before."

"And you claim to have lived on your own for more than a decade."

"I have."

Right. "You have a housekeeper and a maid for a penthouse apartment in a posh building that comes with access to an onsite chef and laundry service."

"So?"

She wiped down counters while he finished loading the dishwasher. "So, you're a dab hand at rinsing dishes and you aren't going to convince me the maid, much less the housekeeper, leaves them in the sink for you to deal with."

"I went to university for four years here, as well as two additional to get my MBA." He put a soap tab in the door and shut the appliance with practiced efficiency. "That is six years doing my own laundry and dishes."

Leaning back against the counter by the sink, she asked, "You didn't live on campus?"

"The first year, yes, and that only meant I didn't have to do my own cooking. My second year, I moved into an apartment with Demyan."

"And you didn't have a housekeeper?" She couldn't imagine Demyan doing anything for himself, either, honestly.

"We both wanted our privacy."

Young college men, sowing their wild oats? That was more understandable than she wanted it to be.

"It was good for you."

"It was. Not everyone living in Volyarus is born in a palace. I need to understand the lives of my people if I am going to make decisions that best serve them." He shrugged out of his suit jacket, hanging it over the back of the kitchen chair.

"You think living without servants for six years helped you do that?"

His tie followed, draped neatly over the top. "That and the time I have spent living with different families throughout Volyarus in the summers, each one with a different job from a different walk of life."

"Wow. I wouldn't have guessed." Her voice went up an octave as he unbuttoned his shirt, exposing his snugly fitting undershirt. "I'm surprised your parents allowed it."

"They insisted on it. My father did the same and his father before him." He kept the shirt on, but there could be no question how he expected their evening to end.

She didn't call him on it because she wasn't entirely sure the confrontation would end up with a victory on her side.

So, she ignored his blatant gestures of intent. "That's kind of amazing."

"And may well be impossible for our own children. Security issues grow increasingly bleak."

"The world is too connected." In years past, a mostly unknown country and its monarchy would have found their first form of defense in their very anonymity.

The internet and a new level of paparazzi that catered to it ensured no one of *any* note remained entirely anonymous in today's world.

"For the freedom we once knew in Volyarus, yes it is." He leaned negligently against the wall beside the built-in desk where she paid her bills.

Feeling unsettled, she moved around the kitchen, rearranging things on the counter, checking the timer on the dishwasher, and avoiding his gaze if she could help it. "Now, you're forced to live the life of a royal because if you don't, you could be kidnapped."

It was a disturbing thought and quickly morphed to the realization her child would be facing the same risks in the future.

"Or assassinated."

A cold chill passed down her spine and Gillian stopped abruptly to face him. "Don't say that."

"Now you know how I feel when you make similar pronouncements about our baby."

"I didn't mean to upset you with the truth."

"Nor I you."

"Okay, fine. I get it. No more mentioning the possibility of miscarriage."

"And marriage?" he asked, with a hopeful charm she found utterly irresistible, but then what about this man wasn't to her?

"On a cruise ship?"

"If you don't like the idea, we can come up with another."

"No. I like it." Too much.

"Ariston will be pleased." Maks grinned, showing the man very pleased was himself.

"You've already approached him?"

"I'm an efficient man, Gillian. You know this."

"Yes, but..."

"Ariston has had his own marital challenges. He is only too happy to help."

Gillian wondered what a Greek shipping tycoon would consider "marital issues" but was too wrapped up in her own at the moment to ask.

"I want Nana and Papa there."

"Absolutely."

"The prenup isn't going to be pretty."

He tried to look all serious, but the grin lurking in his eyes and flirting with the corner of his lips was unmistakable. "Be aware that any assurances you ask for from me, I will demand from you as well."

"No problem."

He nodded, like he hadn't expected any other answer.

She took a deep breath and gave in to the inevitable. "I'll marry you."

Because when it came down to it, she would not deny their child its birthright. But also because she loved him. Because he was committed to making their marriage work in a way a lot of men in love weren't.

Because her future had too bleak a cast without him in it.

"Thank you." He reached into his pocket and pulled out the familiar blue box.

"You knew."

He flipped open the box, revealing the ring so perfect for her. "I hoped, but I had a backup plan."

"What was it?" Seduction probably.

"My mother."

Gillian felt her eyes widen. Some backup plan. That was a woman who could and had been ruthless for the sake of her family and country.

"I'm glad it didn't come to that."

Maks laughed as he removed the ring and set the small blue box aside. "She's not that bad."

"She's a heck of a lot scarier than Demyan."

"I do not think so." He smiled and reached for Gillian, his intention to put the ring on her finger clear.

She flinched back without thought, the inexplicable urge to avoid him overwhelming.

Maks looked gobsmacked. "I cannot touch you?"

"I..." She didn't know why she'd shied from him this time.

His eyes narrowed. "You are not adverse to my touch."

"I don't think I am."

He began moving forward, his expression predatory. "You are not."

"But—"

He put his finger on her lips, pressing with gentle firmness. "No. Our separation has caused you to withdraw from me. Now I will bring you back into the sun."

"You are not the sun."

"But you are a flower about to bloom again." The

naughty look in his espresso dark eyes gave all sorts of connotations to his words.

"Stop trying to sound like a desert sheikh."

He laughed. "I assure you, I am very content to be Volyarussian."

Of that, she had absolutely no doubt.

No man was as proud of his heritage as Crown Prince Maksim of the House of Yurkovich. Part of her craved physical closeness with this dynamic man, and yet Gillian felt this inexplicable urge to push Maks away.

She tried to will her body to relax, but the muscles in her back and neck were rigid with no hope of releasing the tension.

Maks's eyes narrowed and his hands landed very deliberately on her shoulders. Her body tightened, her first instinct to jerk away from him again, but she managed not to give in to it.

He advanced and she backed up, could not help doing so, until she was up against the refrigerator.

Her breath came out in short, near-panicked pants.

He trailed one finger down her throat until it rested over her rapidly beating pulse. "This reaction is excessive, don't you think?"

"Yes." She did; she just didn't know how to fix it.

Their bodies were so close she could feel the heat coming off his. In the past, that heat had always excited or comforted her.

She'd loved it when he spent the night, thinking that he could have kept her warm on even the coldest nights in her Alaskan hometown.

Now, his hotter body temperature made her feel trapped, even marked by his nearness.

She did not understand it.

His fingertip brushed back and forth over her pulse point. "Your body shies from my touch and reacts with alarm to my nearness."

"I don't know why." Only maybe she did.

His leaving had devastated her, left her hurting in a way even her parents' ongoing rejections never had. Her atavistic reaction to him was that of one animal mauled by another.

Even if the mauling had been purely emotional and equally unintentional, she understood that now it had left her entire being wary of this man.

He could not guess at the depths of her pain because he did not truly understand the terrible power of her love. He was right about one thing, though, that power had not been a positive force in her life yet.

And only she could change that.

She'd thought it was all on him. His rejection. His lack of love for her.

But she should have fought for him. If she wanted him and she so did. Only she'd learned way too young that fighting for some things was futile.

"I tried. It didn't work."

"What did you try, *mýla moja?*"

The Ukrainian *my dear* touched her when she wasn't sure she was ready to be touched, reached her heart where she wasn't sure she was ready to be reached. "To get my parents to love me, to want me."

"Even if I refuse to give love room in my life, I want you, Gillian. I always will."

Could he promise that? His expression said he could and he would. She wasn't so sure, but she wanted to believe so much, that it was another, sharper pain to add to the dull ache that never left.

"You thought that by being as perfect as you could be, you would make them want to be with you," he guessed, his dark gaze filled with more understanding than he should be capable of.

"Yes, but it backfired. They thought I was well-adjusted without them. Even my grandparents never understood how painful Rich and Annalea's absence from my life was. Annalea even touts me as an example of what making rational choices can do for everyone involved."

"She believed it was best for all of you for her to abdicate her role as your mother."

"That's what she says."

His espresso gaze searched hers. "It would have been kinder to allow you to be adopted."

"Nana would not hear of it. She insisted on raising me. She and Papa love me, even if they won't claim me as their own."

"They have never denied you."

"Not as a granddaughter, no."

"But they do not consider you their daughter, though they raised you."

"They can't."

"It would mean admitting your father, the son they love, is not the man they choose to believe him to be."

His understanding shocked her until she realized that in Maks's family, he had plenty of experience with the exact same dilemma. "Yes."

"Even so, you are still a fighter."

She wanted to break eye contact, but couldn't. "About other things."

"Important things." There was a strange inflection in his voice when he said the word *important* she couldn't interpret.

"Important yes, but not *all*-important." Would he understand the distinction?

His dark brows drew together and she knew she'd have to spell it out for him. She didn't mind so much, now.

"I called in sick and cried continuously for three days after you left my apartment that morning." She managed to look away, not wanting to see his reaction to her admission. "I've had nightmares only to wake up and realize they were memories."

"That is..." His words trailed off as if this master communicator was at a loss for words.

"It's what people who have suffered a debilitating loss do."

"I did not die."

"Our relationship did." She looked back at him, needing him to see she spoke absolute truth. "I'd lost you. Had no hope of you returning."

"And yet you did not call me as soon as you realized you were pregnant." Confusion clouded his expression.

"I knew you'd insist on marriage and chances were, I would not be strong enough to say no."

"There is no weakness in doing what is best for our child despite what you believe it may cost you."

"The weakness comes in how much I want it," she admitted. "I didn't want to trap you."

"I do not feel trapped." He swallowed, his jaw taut with tension. "I never intended to hurt you that way."

"I believe you."

"Nevertheless, I did it."

"Yes." Because he didn't love her, he could not have guessed at what losing him would cost her.

"I will not leave you again." It was a vow, accompanied by the slipping of the ring on to her finger.

Even though it was prompted by her pregnancy and the fact she now carried the heir to the Volyarus throne, the promise in his voice poured over the jagged edges of her heart with soothing warmth. The small weight of the metal band and diamonds on her finger was a source of more comfort than she would ever have believed possible.

She was not sure her heart would ever be whole again, but it did not have to hurt like it had been for ten weeks.

"I won't leave you, either."

"I know." A small sound, almost a sigh, escaped his mouth. "Now we must convince your body that it still belongs to me."

"You have a very possessive side."

"This is nothing new."

"Actually, it kind of is." He'd shown indications of a possessive nature when they were dating, but he'd never been so primal about it before. "You're like a caveman."

His smile was predatory, his eyes burning with sensual intent. "You carry my child. It makes me feel *very* possessive, takes me back to the responses of my ancestors."

Air escaped her lungs in an unexpected *whoosh.* "Oh."

"I have read that some pregnant women desire sex more often than usual."

"I…" She wasn't sure what she felt in that department right now.

She always seemed to want him and could not imagine her hormones increasing that all too visceral need.

"However, I had not realized the pregnancy could impact the father in the same way." There was no mistaking his meaning.

Maks wanted her. And not in some casual, sex as physical exercise way. The expression in his dark eyes said he wanted to devour her, the mother of his child, sexually.

Gillian shivered in response to that look.

"Cold?" he purred, pushing even closer. "Let me warm you."

"I'm not co—" But she wasn't allowed to finish the thought.

His mouth covered hers in a kiss that demanded full submission and reciprocation.

Her body, the same body that had shied away from his every touch, now capitulated without a single conscious thought on her part. She sank into him while her mouth softened under his, allowing him immediate access to the interior.

Like the marauder his ancestors had been, he took advantage, his tongue seeking hers out with sensual intent. The hand on her throat slid down to her shoulder and then lower to cup her breast.

Sensitive from the hormones running rampant through her body, she felt that initial touch through her pajama top to the very core of her. Gasping against his lips, she pressed into his hand.

His triumphant growl was both animalistic and unbearably exciting.

This man might have all the urbanity expected of a prince on the outside, but underneath beat the heart of a ruthless Cossack. He wanted nothing less than *everything.*

She understood that finally, in absolute clarity. It wasn't enough for him to put a ring on her finger and name her his princess. No, this man would hold absolute possession of her body, would demand nothing less than complete loyalty of her mind and the heart he eschewed interest in.

And God help her, she'd promised to give it.

Not in so many words, but agreeing to marry him

carried with it all sorts of ramifications she hadn't even considered ten weeks ago.

Another shiver rolled through her and the hand still on her shoulder tightened before moving to her bottom. That big, masculine hand curved over her backside, squeezing, proclaiming ownership without a single word.

Then she was being tugged even closer, their bodies as intimate as they could get with clothes on.

His hardened sex pressed into her stomach, his thigh insinuated between her legs to press against her. Pleasure shot through her from the slight stimulation to her clitoris, the position that was both protective and undeniably sexual.

Her own hands found their way to his neck and into the silky, mahogany hair at the back of his head. She tugged on the strands, not to move his head away, but simply because she couldn't help herself.

He responded by deepening the kiss and flexing the leg between her thighs, using his hand on her bottom to maneuver her against his leg and increasing the stimulation to her clitoris almost unbearably.

She wanted to be naked, but couldn't stop kissing Maks long enough to tell him so.

His hand on her bottom kneaded the flesh there, moving inexorably toward her inner thigh and pulling her higher onto his leg at the same time.

Small bursts of pleasure exploded inside her with every small movement. She wasn't even sure she wouldn't climax before they ever got their clothes off.

He seemed intent on bringing her as much pleasure as possible in as short a time as he could. It was not his usual technique.

But then he'd said he was feeling desperate for her, hadn't he?

She didn't know if it was the pheromones coming off her body because of her pregnancy, or if he was simply feeling the separation of ten weeks and his celibacy over that time. And she didn't care.

This grittily passionate lovemaking was exactly what Gillian needed.

She needed him *not* to treat her like fragile glass because she carried his child. She needed to *feel* his desire for *her* to the deepest recesses of her soul.

CHAPTER NINE

GILLIAN HAD COMMITTED to a lifetime with this man without his love.

Knowing his passion for her was strong and imperative gave her hope for their future together.

His hand found its way under her sleeping T-shirt to the unfettered breast beneath. He brushed his fingers over her achingly hard nipple before cupping the flesh around it.

She moaned, no thought of hiding even a smidge of her reaction to him.

In this, at least, there was gut level honesty and an undeniable connection between them and she hoped always would be.

It wasn't love, but it wasn't merely lust, either. Not when her love was so consuming and his sense of possessive connection so overdeveloped.

He lightly pinched her nipple and she cried out against his marauding mouth.

He broke the kiss to laugh in triumph. "You are mine."

"You are even more arrogant than I knew."

Espresso eyes glittered down at her. "Admit it. This baby in your womb and the woman who carries it, you are both *mine.*"

"Yes, we're yours, but you'd better remember that comes with a lot of responsibility for our welfare and I'm not talking about providing materially for us." She had a job and could support herself just fine.

"I know." His handsome face set in serious lines. "You believe I will hurt you as my father has my mother all these years, but it will not happen."

"Your father could never have hurt your mother like you can hurt me." Not even if his mother *had* felt some type of love for King Fedir when she demanded marriage in exchange for a child.

Maks's eyes flared in surprise and then narrowed in understanding. "Because you love me."

"Yes."

If Queen Oxana had loved King Fedir as much as Gillian loved Maks, she would not have forced him into the sordid life of a married man carrying on an affair with his one true love.

His happiness would have been paramount. Just as Maks's happiness was for Gillian.

If she thought marrying him would hurt him, she would refuse to do it. Of that she was absolutely certain. She knew her own heart and what it was capable of. She had a lifetime of testing and stretching it.

"You won't stop saying it because I do not return the sentiment?" Maks asked as his hands and hard thigh continued pushing so much pleasure into her body she thought she might explode with it.

"Do you care if I do?" she gasped out.

For a split second in time he went still, unmistakable vulnerability flashing before it disappeared. "I find that I do."

"I won't stop saying it." Who knew? One day, he might even truly understand what she meant when she did.

She could only hope he'd learn through feelings for her and not someone else.

"Stop it," he ordered, his voice harsh.

"What?"

"You are doing that thing again, that pessimistic thinking."

"How can you possibly know?"

"You get this look on your face, like all joy is in danger of being sucked from your life."

She dropped her gaze, not wanting the level of insight this man was capable of at that moment. "Don't be ridiculous."

He let out a frustrated sound and then his head lowered again, not to kiss her but to launch a sensual onslaught onto her vulnerable neck.

Delight spiraled through her as he reminded her he knew exactly how to bring her, Gillian Harris, the maximum sexual reaction.

And just like that, she was on the verge of climaxing again. This time, he didn't allow for conversation, or interruption, taking her up and over that pinnacle of pleasure without ever directly stimulating her clitoris.

She screamed out her pleasure, no hope of holding the sound in as her body shook in convulsions so powerful they should have been able to shatter bone.

Afterward, he stripped her naked, right there in the kitchen, and tore off his own clothes, before pushing her up against the wall. He lifted her legs, using the power of his muscular six-foot-four-inch frame to hold her in place as he spread her legs wide.

His erection pressed against her entrance, the bulbous tip spreading tender tissues for his invasion.

He paused there, the muscles of his neck corded with the strain of holding back. "You are the only woman I have ever had sex with without a condom between us."

"Even when you were young and stupid?" she gasped out as his erection pushed inside a single slow inch.

"I was young once, never that stupid."

"You never worried about diseases with me."

"I saw your medical records."

"Not stupid."

"Do you want honesty?"

"Always."

"It never entered my mind."

He hadn't even considered the possibility. That made her warm deep inside.

She smiled. "Good."

"Impractical."

"I won't tell."

He laughed, the sound strained. "I know. You would die of embarrassment."

"I'm not sure I can face Demyan as it is."

"You can." Then whatever restraint Maks had been under seemed to break and he pushed all the way inside with a single powerful thrust.

The sound of satisfaction that came from deep in his chest sent another wave of desire crashing over the first one caused by finally having the connection of full intercourse.

Whatever veneer of civility still intact over Maks's features and actions disintegrated in that moment and he began to make love to her with animalistic intensity. His powerful body pistoned in and out of hers, bringing intense pleasure with every potent thrust.

His breath came in harsh gasps, hers no better.

"Never again," he ground out between clenched teeth as he swiveled his hips on the next thrust, causing her clitoris to pulse with pleasure.

She agreed, not sure what she was agreeing to, but hearing the need for her accord in thought in the two words. "Never again."

"Ten weeks is too long."

Without sex. She understood and though she wished he needed her emotionally with the same intensity, his sexual need was its own type of relationship guarantee.

"Come for me again," he demanded as his body possessed hers so completely she would never again doubt who she belonged to.

Not that *she* had ever really been in doubt.

She said nothing, though, too intent on how her body seemed perfectly able to accede to his demand. The wonderful tension built inside, tightening, tightening, tightening…until it released with another life altering culmination.

This time, he came with her, his sex first swelling inside her, pushing her own pleasure toward the edge of unbearable before she felt the heat of his orgasm inside her.

He buried his face in the join of her neck and shoulder, his muscular chest rising and falling with harsh breaths as he repeated a single word over and over. *"Moja."*

Mine.

And though there'd been nothing gentle about this coupling, the profundity she'd felt that night ten weeks ago washed over Gillian again, bringing tears to sting her eyes.

She did not know how he knew, but suddenly Maks's head came up and he searched her face, his own expression unreadable. "Too much?"

"No," she denied.

"Why the tears?"

"I can't explain."

"Pregnancy hormones."

"Maybe," she hedged.

His eyes narrowed. "I wonder."

He lifted her left hand to his lips, kissing right above the ring he'd placed there, the message of possession in his dark gaze unmistakable and undeniable.

Then the gentleness came. He withdrew from her body, carefully lowering her legs to the floor. But he did not leave her to stand on her own; he simply changed his hold and lifted her again.

This time he cradled her against his chest and carried her through to the bathroom. Nothing like the master bath in his penthouse, her bathtub was barely big enough for one. There was no hope of them bathing together unless they showered.

And somehow she knew that was not his plan.

But she didn't want to let go of the connection. She'd learned her lesson about clinging early in life, though, so she said nothing as he lowered her to the side of the tub.

He turned on the tap, adding her favorite bath salts. She watched the level rise, glad for his unconscious hand on her thigh as he swirled the salts so they melted into the hot water.

"The smell of rosemary reminds me of you."

"Isn't that the way it works? Rosemary for remembrance?"

"It's the scent of your bath salts. Rosemary and mint. I like it."

He'd said so before and she'd stopped buying other fragrances for her bath. She didn't admit that now, though. "I like it, too," was all she said.

He nodded before gently lifting her and placing her with what could be mistaken for tender care into the tub.

"I don't need this kind of help," she protested. "I'm pregnant, not helpless."

"We have just made the most passionate of love. I will see to your comfort if I like."

"You're kind of bossy."

"You're *very* independent."

"If you were looking for a leech, you shouldn't have dated me."

"I do not want a leech. A little clinging wouldn't hurt, though," he grumbled under his breath.

She couldn't believe her ears. "Men like you hate women who cling."

"I do not know where you come by your vast knowledge of men like me." He frowned down at her, even as he began to wash her body with a bar of glycerin soap and gentle caresses. "But *I* would enjoy *you* clinging."

"You wouldn't."

"Allow me to know my own mind."

"You get very formal in your speech when you are annoyed, did you know that?"

"It has been mentioned."

"Good, I wouldn't want you to be ignorant of a tell that could hinder your diplomatic or business negotiations."

"For my country they are often one and the same."

"For most countries, I think that's the case."

"You may well be right." He continued to wash her. "You're still bossy."

"It is a trait you are more than capable of withstanding."

"You have a lot of faith in me."

"I chose you for my princess. Of course I do."

And though he'd rejected her it hadn't been for reasons to do with her character. "The world is very black and white for you, isn't it?"

"I know what I must do. I know what I want. I know how to go after both." He settled on the large fluffy rug she kept beside the bath and then continued to wash her as if every single toe and finger needed his undivided attention.

"Am I something you want as well as something you must do?" she asked, not sure she wanted the answer.

"You can ask that after what happened not ten minutes past?"

"This is me clinging."

Incredibly, he smiled. Lifting his head, so she could see the expression had reached his gorgeous eyes, he nodded once. "Good. Yes. I want you. Very much."

It wasn't love, but it was better than pure duty.

Maks held Gillian in his arms, her body lax in sleep, her features soft and vulnerable as they would not be awake.

The sun had risen thirty minutes ago and his schedule for the morning was tight, but he had not gotten up.

He could not help feeling like he'd narrowly averted disaster. Even more disconcerting was his inability to identify how he'd done it.

He did not know why Gillian had agreed to marry him.

No question, she'd taken their baby's welfare to heart. And she said she still loved Maks, but neither gelled in his mind as the reason for her reversal on her stance about agreeing to marry him before she hit her second trimester.

Was it the sex?

The physicality between them was explosive, but was it enough to push her over that mental precipice she'd been balancing on?

He was grateful she had agreed to marry him without doubt, but Maks did not like when the motives of others were cloudy to him. Perhaps it was the way he'd been raised, or his position, but it was never enough to simply know, he had to know *why.*

His life fit into neatly ordered compartments; it always had. The one where Gillian resided had been destroyed ten weeks ago when Maks read the results of her yearly medical examination. Her agreement to marry should have created a new compartment that he could understand and rely on.

It hadn't.

The compartment he had marked for his wife was no longer defined and measurable. And while that made him uncomfortable, he could not regret Gillian's willingness to align her life with his.

Though he found it hard to admit, even to himself, she filled empty places in his life he hadn't realized existed. He was not entirely convinced those places were not supposed to remain empty.

The last months had been hollow in a way his life never was before the recognition that his role and responsibilities might not be enough.

One night of incredible sex, a few days of *connection*

and that hollowness was gone. The possibility it could return made something tighten in his chest.

He was never letting this woman out of his life again.

She thought the prenuptial agreement was for her protection, but he was as eager to have her sign it as she was to take measures to protect the future of their family. Unlike his parents, or her own, theirs would be a real marriage for a lifetime.

Sliding his hand down her arm, he let it come to rest over hers, the large square-cut diamond of her engagement ring pressing into his palm, giving him a deep sense of satisfaction.

The expensive piece of jewelry marked her as his, but not as primally, and therefore satisfyingly as the passion mark he'd left on her breast, or the slight razor burn on her neck that evidenced his passion of the night before.

The desire to own and be owned surged through him.

Yes, he was a possessive guy. He would be king; absolute allegiance was something he'd been taught to give and expect.

What shocked him was the equally strong desire for others and Gillian herself to acknowledge that he was hers. Her fiancé, soon to be her husband.

The father of her child, the one and only man she would ever expend her passion on.

"What have you woken up thinking about?" she asked, her voice laced with amusement and sleepy desire.

"What do you mean?" he hedged.

She shifted slightly so his hardened sex rubbed against her hip. "What do you think I mean?"

"Oh, that."

"Yes. *That.*" She laughed, the sound so pleasing his erection jumped against her hip.

"My desire for you is nothing new."

"No, it isn't." She turned so her beautiful blue eyes could meet his. "I like it."

"I also."

"Want to do something about it?" she asked with a comical leer.

It was his turn to laugh, the sound going from his mouth to hers as he claimed her lips with a ferocity only this woman had ever sparked in him.

Their lovemaking was passionate and drawn out, Gillian giving as good as she got, and Maks had reason to appreciate her agreement to be his wife once again.

Afterward, she cuddled in his arms, clinging as she so rarely allowed herself to do and in a way he found himself craving more with each passing day.

As much as he enjoyed the moment, he could not prolong it. His day's schedule had been set before he'd arrived at her apartment the night before and he would already have to cancel the phone conference he had planned for before his early morning flight.

With more regret than he wanted to admit to, even to himself, he pulled away to get out of the bed. "I have to fly to Volyarus this morning."

It was not lost on him that she made no effort to hold him back. Gillian was no doubt correct that many men like him would find that reaction a relief from their lover. He would have been one with any other lover before her, but she was more than the woman who shared his bed.

Gillian Harris was the woman he had chosen to spend his life with.

For all her claims to love him, she did not act like a woman whose happiness depended on his presence. In any way.

He did not like the suspicion that he might find her presence in his life more necessary than she found his.

She sat up, pulling the sheet and comforter with her as she did so, maintaining a modesty unnecessary between them.

But strangely appealing nonetheless.

Was there *anything* about this woman he did not find attractive? Her lack of clinginess notwithstanding, he could not think of one.

"Okay." She tucked her blond hair behind her ear. "You'd better take a shower then."

"You could ask when I have to leave, or how long I plan to be gone." Did she not have even the most rudimentary interest in his plans?

Her brows furrowed and Gillian's head canted to one side. "You want me to quiz you on your schedule? Wouldn't it just be easier to sync our calendars?"

Annoyance surged through him. "You're very tech-oriented for an artist."

"What can I say? I love my smartphone, but you know that."

"Yes." He should have gotten her the newest one on the market instead of a ridiculously expensive ring from Tiffany's.

"Whatever you're thinking isn't very nice. I think you'd better keep it to yourself."

"You think you can read my mind?" he scoffed.

"Your expression isn't exactly stealthy right now."

Affronted, he drew himself to his full impressive height. "My ability to hide my thoughts is second to none."

He'd been training at it since birth.

"When you're making an effort, yes, it is."

"Perhaps I have allowed myself to become too relaxed around you."

"We're going to be married." Her brows furrowed and her lips formed a straight line. "I don't think I would like it if you hadn't."

"Oh." He had not considered that angle. "My parents are not trusted confidants to one another."

"We have already established that we are not going to emulate them in important ways."

"And this is one of those ways?"

"Absolutely."

He nodded, accepting that she expected a similar level of trust to what he gave his cousin.

Shockingly the prospect did not bother him. "I would like you to go with me."

"This morning?" she asked, her expression not promising.

"Yes."

"I have a full schedule today and tomorrow for that matter."

"You work too much."

"It would be pretty hard to pay the bills otherwise."

"You are no longer alone."

"What, we get engaged and suddenly I'm supposed to quit my job and let you *take care* of me?" The scathing tone left no doubt what she thought of that idea.

"Not quit, no, but cut back? I would prefer it. Wouldn't your doctor?"

"She made no stipulations about my work. It's not physical enough to be risky to my pregnancy."

"You are tired."

"Not right now." But her honest blue eyes told their own story.

"You would like to cut back your hours," he guessed.

"I'm not lazy."

"No, you are not."

"You don't expect me to quit?"

"No."

"Even after we are married?"

"Photography gives you a great deal of satisfaction. There is no reason you should give it up entirely."

"What part should I give up?" she asked in a wary tone he did not understand.

"I do not know. Whatever assignments are not as interesting to you?" Communication with women had always been like navigating a minefield for Maks.

He had hoped with Gillian agreeing to be his wife,

it would be more straightforward, less fraught with explosive traps.

"You don't have any particular ones in mind?"

"No."

"My father disparages my book covers and is barely more tolerant of my portraits, but they at least have some artistic merit in his eyes."

"I am not your father. And your portraits are pure and amazing art. I am no expert in the industry, but I like your book covers as well." Maks had seen Gillian's portfolio.

Her photographic portraiture was indeed unique. He was actually quite surprised it didn't dominate her work and had remarked on that fact in the past.

She'd told him her prices were very high for the portraits she did do and she was really picky about what clients she took on. She wasn't nearly as choosy about her book covers.

She brought other people's visions to life with them. For her, it was a different kind of art. Apparently equally satisfying, but different.

"You just want me to cut back my hours?" she asked cautiously.

"The life of a princess is not without its demands. Your body is already taxed with the pregnancy."

"How long do you plan to be in Volyarus?"

"Two weeks. I should have left several days ago."

"But then Demyan told you about our little problem."

"Our baby is not a problem."

"No, I didn't mean it that way."

"Good."

"You're awfully touchy."

"I am going to be late." He turned toward the bath-room. "Go back to sleep. It is still early."

CHAPTER TEN

"Bossy," Gillian muttered as Maks left the room.

She wasn't really sure why the conversation had ended so abruptly. He'd thrown his need to leave and desire for her to accompany him out there and barely given her a chance to respond before dismissing her and what they'd been talking about.

True, he hadn't left the apartment, but he'd effectively left the conversation, *with instructions for her to sleep.*

One thing Nana always said was that a woman who intended to enjoy her future had to begin as she meant to go on in any relationship. Whether of short or long duration, it was always worth setting expectations.

Their marriage would definitely fall under the long duration header.

Throwing back the covers, Gillian climbed out of the bed, glad the morning nausea that had plagued her seemed to be tapering off. She went to grab a robe, but then put it back deliberately. The water was already running for the shower.

He would just have to share.

It wouldn't be super comfortable, but they'd done it before.

The bathroom was already filling up with steam from the hot shower when she reached it.

"You're going to have to share the hot water," she announced as she pulled back the shower curtain far enough for her to step into the tub with him.

He turned around quickly, his expression reflecting surprise.

She barely refrained from rolling her eyes. "Did you really think you could just tell me to go back to sleep and I would do it?"

"You need your rest."

"We weren't done discussing the things you'd brought up."

"I thought we were."

"Really?"

"Yes." The exasperation in his tone would have been more impacting if his dark gaze wasn't devouring her nudity.

"We made love twice last night."

"So?"

"So, you look like you're thinking about doing it again."

"I am, but there isn't time." His tone was laden with unmistakable regret.

She laughed softly. "I don't remember you being this insatiable."

"Don't you?"

Actually, he'd never made his fascination with her

body a secret. "You're more primitive about it now. I feel like you have this need to mark me."

Incredibly, color washed across his cheekbones and then concern darkened his eyes. "Was I too rough?"

"No. Not at all. I like this less civilized side."

"That is good to know."

She put shower gel on a loofah and began washing him. "So, you want me to come to Volyarus."

"My mother will want to see you." He made a soft sound of pleasure in the back of his throat as she brushed the loofah over his chest.

"Will she be angry?"

"That you are not with me?"

She shook her head at this masculine inanity. "That we have to get married."

"She approved my choice ten months ago."

"Oh." Gillian hadn't realized it had gone as far as Maks talking his choice of a wife over with his mother. "My medical results certainly threw a spanner in the works for you."

"Temporarily."

She shook her head. "You really are an optimist, aren't you?"

"I think you need that."

"To counterbalance my so-called pessimism?" she asked sarcastically, her hands falling away from him.

His expression was entirely serious when he said, "Yes."

"I'm not a pessimist."

"Then you do a very good imitation of one."

"People say hope doesn't cost anything, but that's not true. When you hope for things and you are disappointed, it hurts. When it happens a lot, hope gets harder and harder to let in." She began washing herself, scrubbing with the loofah with jerky movements.

He reached to her, tugged the loofah from her hand and hung it from the hook on the enclosure wall, and then pulled her gently into his body. "I will do my best to fulfill the hopes you allow room in your heart."

"You're awfully poetic for a Cossack." Tears tightened her throat.

"I'm not a Cossack."

"Your ancestors were and sometimes genetics ring true."

"Do they? What hope does our child have then?" he teased.

Gillian opined firmly, "She will have the best of both of us."

"Was that optimism I heard?" He put his hand over his heart, feigning shock.

She smacked his chest, but gave a hiccupping laugh. "Yes."

"Will you be able to join me in Volyarus?" Tension she didn't understand after the humor and the charm came off him in waves.

"I think so. It will mean moving some things around and into the weekend, but then I can join you Monday and stay that week and through the weekend."

"You will do that?"

Gillian tilted her head back so their eyes met. This

needed to be said. He deserved to know she understood the differences that being his wife would make in her life. "Maks, I know that marrying you comes with a job title."

"Princess."

"It's an honor." That he'd wanted to give her ten weeks ago.

He grimaced. "But not one you aspired to."

"No, but I always knew it would be necessary if I was to remain in your life permanently."

"And did you have plans to do so, before?"

"You know I did."

"You would have agreed to my proposal ten weeks ago."

"If you'd made one, yes, I would have." She wasn't going to lie to him.

"But you had no intention of accepting my proposal when I made it four days ago."

"You know why."

He frowned, looking like he wanted to say no he didn't, but was manfully refraining.

She couldn't help laughing, though her humor might be more macabre than jolly. "I know. You don't understand the fear that love might bring."

"I thought the saying was perfect love casts out fear."

"I'm not perfect and neither is my love."

"On that we must disagree."

"What?" Now *she* was totally confused.

He pulled her closer, their naked flesh fitting together so naturally under the cascading hot water that emotion choked her. "You are perfect for me."

"Because I carry your child."

"That's part of it, yes, but then even that only shows how insanely compatible we are. No one else could have gotten you pregnant in a single night without condoms."

"Conceited much?"

"No. This isn't about my prowess...it's about how we fit." He was very serious, his espresso eyes filled with sincerity.

To hear his words describing the feeling that had been washing over her touched something deep inside, something she thought would always hurt. Only right now, the pricks and stings were absent.

It was not love, but it was something.

She buried her face against his chest, needing a moment, but he refused to let her hide from him. Even for a second. He tilted her head up the same time he lowered his mouth to hers and pressed their lips together in the gentlest kiss.

Tenderness remained, but the gentleness quickly morphed into something else. A passion that coursed through her, making her heart beat so fast she could barely catch her breath.

They were both breathing heavily, the steam around them not as hot as their bodies had become when he moved to kiss down her throat.

"I thought we didn't have time," she gasped.

"I already missed one meeting." His hand slid down her backside and between her thighs, his fingertips playing over the slick flesh. "My pilot will have to wait as well."

She didn't argue, though she was sure it was more than his pilot that sex would put on hold. He knew it, too. And that just blew her away. Realizing Maks could be distracted from duty for the intimacy between them was more mind-altering than the pleasure they found in one another's bodies.

And that always left her feeling like she'd had an out-of-body experience, or rather a very intense in-body experience.

The need to show how very much that meant to her grew inside Gillian until she became determined to do something she'd never done before. Dropping to her knees, she nuzzled into his lower abdomen, her intentions clear.

Her wet hair brushed over his already hardened sex and he groaned, his hips canting for more contact. The man was insatiable and she was glad. Really, really glad.

No, it wasn't love, but it *was* something worth fighting for.

He sucked in air, another long, low groan pealing out of him as she turned and quite deliberately licked his length.

"What are you doing?" he croaked out.

"If you don't know, I am not doing it right."

"But you don't do this." He'd never asked it of her and she'd never offered.

"It isn't because I don't want to."

"Then why?"

She looked up; able to admit something she wouldn't have even twenty-four hours earlier. "I don't know how."

"You've *never* done it before." He sounded almost awed.

She shook her head. Gillian was determined to do it now, though, as much for herself as for him. She'd always wanted to—with him, but she'd lacked the confidence to try when his sexual history was so much richer than hers.

She didn't just want to try something new, she craved giving him pleasure like he'd never known.

Yesterday she would have doubted her ability to do that, but the day before Prince Maksim of the House of Yurkovich had not been so moved by his desire for Gillian Harris that he'd chosen to circumvent his own schedule.

While he did not make it a habit to cancel on her, he had *never* rearranged his schedule to spend time with her, either. Not once, not even pushing a meeting back by five minutes, much less rescheduling it altogether.

But not only was he purposefully giving up his take-off slot at the airport, Maks had already missed a meeting to spend as much of the morning's early hours with her that he had.

Overwhelmed with a kind of giddy joy at the thought of it, Gillian kissed the weeping tip of his erection, lapping at the moisture. It was sweeter than she expected and she made a sound of approval.

His swollen hardness jumped against her lips. "Put it in your mouth. *Please.*"

"Yes." She took his head into her mouth and wondered how she was supposed to take more.

He wasn't small by any means and her mouth only stretched so wide.

Refusing to worry about the fact she couldn't take it all in, she swirled her tongue around the head, eliciting groans from Maks. He certainly didn't seem to mind she wasn't going to deep throat him like a porn star.

He fell back against the wall of the tub enclosure, his big body giving one long shudder. *"Feels so good."*

She curled both her hands around the wet shaft and began stroking him as she changed her licking to sucking.

He shouted, his hips surging forward as if he could not control the movement.

He penetrated her mouth farther, but her hands on his shaft prevented him from going too far.

"Sorry," he gritted out, making an obvious effort to remain still.

She felt like smiling, happy he'd lost control. It meant he didn't have all the power in their relationship.

Part of her had known that, because she carried his child, but part of her had felt helpless in the face of her own love.

She was feeling anything but helpless right now with his extreme response to her novice, but enthusiastic efforts. Increasing the speed of her caresses, she was surprised at how excited doing this for him made her.

She wanted to bring him off, but she ached with the desire to be filled, too.

She couldn't stop what she was doing to tell him. Didn't want to stop pleasuring him with her mouth. It was such an amazing feeling, to have him at her mercy and yet be so emotionally connected it was like a live current of electricity arced between them.

But he grabbed her head, pulling her back.

She frowned up at him.

His pupils were blown, his face dark with passion and he rasped out, "I'm about to climax."

"I want you to."

He let out a pained groan, his hips flexing. "No. You don't."

"I like the taste."

"Come is not as sweet as preejaculate, or so I've been told."

"Really?" Her frown turned to a glare, some of passion's haze dissipating.

He laughed, the sound almost tortured. "You have nothing to be jealous about. No other woman has ever affected me like you do. No other one ever will."

She believed him. Today. This morning, after he *chose* to miss his takeoff slot to be with her, she believed him.

He tugged gently on her head, both hands on either side of her face and she found herself rising to stand in front of him. "I want to be inside you."

"Y..." Her voice gave out, her own want was so deep. She cleared her throat. *"Yes."*

He kissed her, his mouth laying claim to hers without apology or hesitation.

She kissed him back, asserting her own claim, letting him know with the ferocity of her response that he belonged to her as well.

She didn't know which one of them broke the kiss, or how she ended up facing the far wall of the tub enclosure with her legs spread as much as they could go in the narrow space, her nipples aching in the moist air.

But she literally shook with the need for copulation.

His body blanketed hers, his sex aligned to the apex of her thighs. "Let me have you, *sérdeńko,* open yourself to me."

"Yes!" She threw her head back against his shoulder, a tiny part of her brain insisting she'd find out what *sérdeńko* meant later.

His erection pressed between her legs, zeroing in on the opening to her body and pressing inside in one smooth movement. He filled her, the stretch so perfect, so intense and the angle just right for hitting her G-spot, ecstasy sparked hot along each nerve ending.

One long fingered hand reached around and delved between her folds to tease her clitoris, the other slid up her stomach to play with her breasts. The multiple stimulations were body buzzing and mind numbing.

Her brain stopped making fully realized thoughts as he touched her in ways guaranteed to bring her the ultimate in pleasure and she offered her body to him without limits.

The water beat down on them; Maks moved with

passionate urgency, his sex caressing that sweet spot inside her, his fingertip rubbing circles of delight on her clitoris.

The pleasure spun higher and higher inside of Gillian, her body naturally arching up on her toes in response, her hands against the slick wall in no way holding her up. It was Maks's strength doing that, his big Cossack's body.

And then everything exploded in a starburst of color that rivaled the Northern Lights, her body convulsing around his sex, her womb contracting with ecstasy, her breath sawing in and out in passion-filled pants.

The scream of completion that ripped out of Gillian's throat mixed with Maks's feral shout as he climaxed, too, his body rigid behind her, their voices rising in a crescendo of delight.

As the pleasure ebbed, small aftershocks dwindling to an all over sense of perfect well-being and happiness, she became aware of the small kisses he was placing along her neck, cheek and temple. She turned her head and their lips met in a moment so laden with her love, it was a living blanket around them.

They shared kisses between drying each other off after finishing their shower in lukewarm water. Her apartment didn't have the unlimited hot water tank his swank penthouse suite enjoyed.

"What does *sérdeńko* mean?" she asked.

Maks stilled and then leaned forward to kiss the side of her face. "Heart. It means heart."

It was her turn to pause, everything inside her stilled in wonder. "Why?"

"You are the heart of this relationship."

It wasn't the words of love her soul longed to hear, but it was so much more than she'd expected after the way they'd broken up ten weeks ago, Gillian had to duck her head so he didn't see the moisture pooling in her eyes.

He knew, though. Maks always knew.

He pulled the towel from her unresisting fingers and pulled her into another full body hug. "It will be good between us, Gillian. Believe me."

"I do." For the first time since she was a tiny child, Gillian made no effort to temper the hope bubbling up inside her like the sweetest of champagnes.

CHAPTER ELEVEN

THE NEXT FOUR days were a blur of activity for Gillian as she worked to clear her schedule for the last-minute trip to Volyarus.

Maks video called her twice a day, once in the morning and before bed each night.

In between, he was back to texting her frequently and now she was getting all three meals delivered as well as snacks in between. Some came to her apartment, others her studio, but when the catered delivery showed up at an offsite shoot, she knew this was more than just a matter of Maks instructing someone to make sure she got fed.

He was taking care of her and she liked it. She liked it a lot.

The private jet Maks sent to bring Gillian to Volyarus was swank, every appointment on the luxury end of comfortable. It was also already occupied.

Gillian had only met the woman sitting primly in the leather seat facing the entry door a handful of times, but she would have recognized Queen Oxana even if she never had. The queen of Volyarus might be a lesser known royal in the world of monarchies, but her visage had been in enough magazines and newspaper articles to make her a recognizable figure.

"Good evening, Miss Harris."

Extremely grateful for all the awkward moments she'd spent at her father's side at social functions now, Gillian did a standing curtsy. "Your highness."

The queen rose from her chair, even that small movement graceful and elegant. "You may address me as Oxana. We are to be mother and daughter by marriage, I am told."

Gillian couldn't tell how the older woman felt about that fact from her perfectly smooth tone and politely inquiring features. Where the heck was Maks?

She couldn't believe this little tête-à-tête was his idea. Which meant it was the queen's. Oh, joy.

"Yes." Gillian swallowed, her mouth gone dry.

"You are pregnant with my son's child."

"He told you?" The adrenaline of shock lasted only a few seconds and then tiredness took over, the past weeks catching up to her in an inexorable wave of mental and physical exhaustion. Gillian sighed, putting her bag on the seat nearest her. "Of course he told you."

"Actually he did not."

"Demyan?" Gillian guessed.

"Yes."

"But why?"

"Apparently, unlike my son, he thought I should know the reason for Maksim's insistence on a rushed elopement followed by a State reception." The queen waved toward one of the cream leather seats, indicating Gillian should take it.

Knowing their takeoff slot was approaching quickly, Gillian put her seat belt on as soon as she'd lowered herself to the cushy leather. "Yes, of course. What I meant was why didn't Maks tell you?"

Perfectly tweezed and shaped eyebrows rose slightly. "He does not want me to believe you have trapped him into marriage."

"He's protecting me." Typical but not altogether welcome in this instance. Gillian would much rather Maks'd had this discussion with his mother. "The news was bound to come out."

Queen Oxana nodded as she returned to her own seat, leaving the belt undone. "Yes, it was. Sooner than later and if he was thinking with his usual clarity, he would have realized this."

"I haven't noticed any lack in his sharp brain processes."

"Haven't you?"

"No." Heat washed through Gillian, bringing with it a resurgence of the nausea she'd thought was gone for good.

Suddenly the queen was standing over Gillian, her hand on Gillian's forehead. "You feel a bit clammy. Are you nauseated?"

Gillian could only swallow and nod.

Moments later, Gillian had a glass of carbonated mineral water and soda crackers sitting in front of her.

The queen had returned to her seat, buckling her belt when the engines started warming up.

Gillian nibbled on the soda crackers while taking sips of the mineral water and tried to calm her inexplicably racing heart as the plane began its taxi toward takeoff. Or maybe not so hard to understand in the circumstances. She reacted to her own mother's presence this way.

Why not a queen's?

Queen Oxana spoke quietly to the flight attendant and then the man moved to the back of the cabin. Eyes so like her son's examined Gillian with probing dispassion. At least, it *looked* like a lack of feeling.

Gillian was fairly certain there was a cauldron of emotion under the placid royal exterior.

"Feeling better?" Queen Oxana asked.

"Yes. How did you know, that I wasn't feeling well, I mean?" Since she had been sitting down, there was no way the older woman could have seen how dizzy Gillian had become.

"Your face is quite expressive."

So her urge to throw up had been evident in her expression? How attractive. "I see."

"You will have to work on that."

If she was going to keep up with the queen and her son, Gillian certainly would. Thinking that went without saying and that Maks's mother didn't need Gillian's verbal agreement, she took a sip of her water and considered the next few hours in light of her company.

This led to another sip as her stomach roiled.

She was going to kill Maks. With his Machiavellian brain, he should have realized what Queen Oxana would do and circumvented it.

"I am not certain what that particular expression means, but it seems like someone might be in trouble."

"You could say that."

"My appearance surprised you."

"Yes." There was no point in trying to pretend otherwise. The way Gillian had nearly fainted in her seat was a dead giveaway.

"Maksim was born with duties and expectations few could understand, much less live up to."

Unsure where the queen was going with that statement, Gillian nodded.

"He has always accepted his role without regret or complaint."

"I know." Gillian wished she knew the script for this scenario. "He has a highly developed sense of responsibility."

"Some might even say *over*developed."

"Yes, but I would be surprised if you were one of them."

"I am not the starry-eyed idealist I was when I first became queen. As I have gotten older, I have come to realize that perhaps my son's happiness is as important as his duty to the throne."

Gillian could not stifle the gasp of shock that opinion elicited.

Queen Oxana smiled wryly. "Yes, I know, Maks and

his father both would find the idea bordering on the heretical."

"But…" Gillian realized she did not want to bring up the queen's own choices that precluded happiness for the sake of duty.

The woman might be a public figure, but that did not make her life an open book.

"I would like to ask you a question, and I would appreciate it very much if you would answer honestly. Though I have little confidence you could hide the truth with your open expressions," the queen mused, seemingly appreciative of that fact rather than disparaging.

"All right." Gillian took another careful sip of water, her nausea not noticeably improved yet.

Queen Oxana nodded, like she hadn't expected any other answer. "Did you get pregnant in order to trap my son into marriage?"

Water spewed as Gillian choked on the question and the beverage. The queen pressed a button and the flight attendant came bearing a linen napkin and a fresh glass of water. How he'd procured both so quickly, Gillian was content to leave a mystery.

He left, the damp napkin and her "compromised" glass of water in his capable hands.

"My question shocked you. It upset you as well, I think." Queen Oxana looked vaguely regretful.

Gillian took several deep breaths and frowned at the queen, not even a little appeased. "You think?"

"Sarcasm can be very unpredictable in its outcome when used in a diplomatic setting."

"So can inappropriately probing questions."

"Touché."

"I am not a gold digger."

"Many people find power far more seductive than money."

"The only thing seductive about Maks's life is the fact that he's in it," Gillian said with pure sincerity.

Queen Oxana's eyes widened infinitesimally, the only sign that she might be surprised by Gillian's viewpoint. "Demyan said you did not tell Maksim of your pregnancy."

"Demyan needs a hobby that *isn't* spying on me."

The queen's lips tilted in an almost smile, humor glinting briefly in her dark eyes. "He has not spied on you personally."

Gillian just looked at Queen Oxana, not willing to play a game of words right then. She was at enough of a disadvantage; she wasn't going to let the older woman lure her into engaging in a sparring match Gillian had little hope of winning.

Her experience with the rich and powerful had taught her the effectiveness of silence and reticence.

The queen nodded, as if Gillian had confirmed something though nothing had been said. "Tell me, why did you not inform my son of your pregnancy immediately?"

"I felt it was best to wait."

"Why? Did you hope the further along you were, the more desperate Maksim would be to give his child legitimate claim to its place in the House of Yurkovich?"

"No." What kind of manipulative, self-serving person did this woman think Gillian was?

Depressed emotion overwhelmed her. She'd been feeling so hopeful, but the queen's doubt and clear disapproval despite her calm air renewed Gillian's own worries about this marriage born of necessity, not love.

She kept telling herself that even though they didn't have love, they had something special. How long could the special part of it last though if his mother disapproved and sought to undermine Gillian's relationship with the future king?

Doing her best to swallow the emotion clawing at her, she said, "Eleven weeks ago, your son dumped me because my medical exam revealed that I have compromised fallopian tubes."

No shock showed on the queen's placid features. "Again, Maksim did not share this with me."

"But you knew anyway."

"Naturally. Demyan did not learn his habits from a stranger."

"Was that a joke?" If it was, Gillian wasn't laughing.

Queen Oxana flashed that barely there smile again. "Perhaps."

When Gillian made no effort to continue the conversation, the queen remarked, "I have yet to understand why you hesitated to tell my son of your condition."

"It's not a condition. It's a baby."

"I apologize. I did not intend to offend you."

No? Gillian just shook her head. "You and my birth mother would get along well."

"In that, I think you are mistaken." For a moment, unmistakable emotion clouded the queen's eyes and it wasn't humor.

There was no question that for some reason, the queen of Volyarus did not like the feminist politician from South Africa.

"If you say so."

"It truly was not my intention to offend."

"I find that hard to believe. Your diplomatic skills rival your son's, or so I've been led to believe."

"Perhaps my son is not the only one disturbed by recent events."

Well, that told Gillian where she and the baby in her womb stood in the queen's estimation. They were *disturbing.*

"I didn't tell Maks about our baby because my fallopian tubes are still compromised. If I miscarried, we were in the same place we had been ten weeks ago." Simply saying the words reminded Gillian what she was ignoring in order to marry Maks. "I would once again be the wrong person to be his princess."

"Maksim, in his usual optimistic fashion, ignored that possibility, did he not?"

"Yes."

Queen Oxana seemed to thaw slightly. "Why were you concerned about the viability of your pregnancy?"

"Rates for miscarriage are higher than most people are aware. Stress increases them."

"Having been abandoned by the man you loved would have caused enough of that commodity."

Gillian had never said so to Maks, but yes. She nodded.

"You felt like you were defective and worried that increased your chances of losing this miraculous baby."

Gillian had no idea how the queen came to that conclusion, but she could not deny it. "Yes."

"Maksim has no idea, does he?"

"Of course not. He wouldn't know how to feel defective."

"Thank you."

Gillian found a smile. "Nana would say you raised him right."

"Your grandmother is a very colorful character."

"She is that." Nana was going to add some interesting spice to royal gatherings in Volyarus.

"I, on the other hand, understand intimately that feeling of defectiveness." Sadness shone in Queen Oxana's dark gaze. "I lost three babies after Maksim's birth."

Gillian sucked in a breath. "I'm very sorry."

"Thank you. Some pain is so deep, it never leaves completely."

The fact the royal couple had married in order for Queen Oxana to provide heirs to the throne made the tragedies that much more poignant.

The queen looked out the oversize cabin windows into a rapidly darkening sky. "I would have enjoyed a houseful of children."

It was such an unexpected thing for a woman like the impeccable and controlled queen to say, Gillian gasped.

The older woman looked back at Gillian, meeting

her gaze with a troubled brown gaze. "You cannot pic-
ture it, can you?"

Gillian considered lying, but wouldn't disrespect the
other woman with less than honesty. "Frankly, no."

"The miscarriages, the dissolution of my marriage
in every way but on paper, it all changed me, but one
thing I never lost was my desire for more children. I
never resented Demyan's place in our lives. Far from it."

"Maks considered you a very good mother." No
doubt Demyan had as well.

The man had picked up the queen's habits by her
own admission.

"I am pleased to hear that, but I fear I did him a terrible disservice in raising him so focused on duty and
with such a wariness toward love."

"You know he's only marrying me because of that
deeply ingrained sense of duty, don't you?" Stupid
tears Gillian blamed on pregnancy hormones burned
her eyes. Understandably the queen regretted raising
her son in a way that made the current situation possible. "I know it, too."

No matter how much Gillian might wish things were
different.

"You do not believe my son would have married you
without the baby to draw you together?"

"I know he wouldn't." Hadn't the older woman been
listening when Gillian told her that Maks had broken
up with her eleven weeks ago?

"Maksim has been very attentive the past days he
has been in Volyarus for a man only doing his duty."

"He's a committed guy. I'm one of his responsibilities now." And she'd been an idiot to let herself begin to believe it might be something more.

If not love, something.

Right.

"Surely you do not begin to imagine my son does not care for you?"

She almost snarked back, *surely you don't imagine he does*. Only Maks did care, if only for the fact she was the mother of his unborn child. "Your son does not love me. He's been very clear on that point."

"Has he?" The queen almost looked guilty. "Has he explained why?"

"Can you explain why one person falls in love and another doesn't?" Gillian asked, trying to get hold of her emotions and knowing she hadn't succeeded when her voice came out shaky from the tears she refused to let fall.

"He is afraid to love. I made him that way."

Gillian wouldn't deny that his mother's views on the subject had influenced Maks, but ultimately the problem was with what he actually felt, not what he thought about feeling. "He doesn't believe in love and really, it's a moot point. If he loved me, he wouldn't be able to deny it."

"I think you underestimate my son's power of will."

Gillian shrugged, not agreeing but lacking the energy or will to argue the semantics of emotions with the queen.

She was sure the other woman had something else

of more importance—to her anyway—to discuss. "Is this where you try to buy me off, or something, your highness?"

"I must insist you address me as Oxana. We *will* be family." For once all of the other woman's emotions showed on her perfectly made up features. And every single one of them was horror. "As to your question, no. Absolutely not."

"But you think I trapped your son into marriage."

"No."

"You asked…" Gillian let her voice trail off.

What did it matter? The queen…*Oxana* had only brought to the forefront what Gillian knew in her heart to be true. Maks had been coerced into marriage by his personal sense of honor and his very real concern for their baby. There was no getting around it.

They were both trapped and guilt was like a stone in Gillian's heart because part of her was glad. That had to make her a very selfish person, even though she would never have intentionally pushed Maks into their current situation.

"I want you to marry my son," Oxana said quite distinctly.

"I find that difficult to believe."

"Again, I am sorry. I am not usually so inept at making my wishes known."

Gillian had no trouble believing that.

"I did not like the idea you had tricked Maksim into marriage."

"Like you did his father."

The queen did not react angrily to the supposition, but she shook her head. "There was no trickery involved with Fedir. He wanted my womb. I wanted him."

"Maks believes you only wanted to be queen."

"Maksim sees the best in his parents. It is a child's prerogative."

"Yes, I suppose it is."

"Fedir never stopped loving that woman, even after Maksim was born."

"It didn't work for Leah, either."

For a moment Queen Oxana looked confused, but then her expression cleared. "From the Old Testament? No. I should be grateful that Bhodana never conceived, but I am not. Fedir would have enjoyed having more children."

"I thought the countess was infertile."

"No tests were done. It was her status as a divorcée that prevented her marriage to Fedir while his father still lived."

"And your presence as his wife after."

"He would not dissolve our marriage. He refused even when I offered."

"He and Maks have a warped sense of duty to Volyarus."

"Overdeveloped and maybe it is warped, but I never saw it that way."

"You shared it. After all, you stayed."

"Of course I stayed. My son was to be king one day. He needed me to guide him and Demyan's own parents abandoned him to our care for the sake of their own ambitions. He needed me as well."

"In the end, you're saying it was the children who came first."

"As it should be."

"I agree."

"That is why you are marrying Maksim?"

"Yes."

"You love him."

"With everything in me."

"And that is what makes this so difficult for you? That is what brings the grief and pain into your lovely blue eyes."

"He won't love me." The truth of that statement weighed like an anvil on Gillian's soul. "It's not an emotion that grows out of nothing."

"You have a child between you, common interests, shared experiences. That is not nothing."

"You had all those same things with King Fedir, but he never learned to love you."

"His love was already spoken for."

"It wouldn't have mattered."

"You don't think so? I am not so sure, but I suspect you are right. He cried out her name...the nights we tried for a baby."

It was such a startlingly intimate revelation, Gillian knew it was heartfelt and extemporaneous. "I'm sorry. If Maks did that, I'm not sure he'd leave the bed with his bits intact."

Incredibly Queen Oxana laughed. "As it should be.

Perhaps a good kick in certain regions would have knocked sense in the king."

"Maybe." Love wasn't the great bearer of rationality, though.

"I believe you are wrong."

"About what?"

"My son's feelings for you."

Gillian wished with all her heart she was, but she knew the truth. "No."

Gillian's first view of Volyarus was glittery lights in the extended blackness that was night in the Baltic Sea.

From research she'd done, Gillian knew that while the majority of the inhabitants of the small nation lived on the main island about the size of New Zealand, it was actually an archipelago with some of the most profitable mineral rights existing on the lesser inhabited, more barren islands.

The main island boasted a mountain whose snow peak never melted but at the base of which a thriving capital city was surrounded by extremely productive farm land.

The growing season was short, but the constant sunlight made for bumper crops.

Gillian couldn't see any of that as she stood on the top of the steps leading down from the jet's doorway.

The early summer darkness here was absolute, once the sun had set. Like it had been in Alaska growing up. The landing strip and its surroundings were lit, but the area beyond was nothing but inky blackness.

Three cars waited at the bottom of the stairs. Two SUVs with large unsmiling men standing beside them and an official-looking stretch limousine with the flags of Volyarus flying on either side of the hood. The driver stood by the open back door.

A silver Mercedes sports class, just like the black one Maks drove in Seattle, came screeching to a halt on the tarmac as Gillian reached the bottom of the steps shortly after the queen.

"Oh, dear," Oxana said. "It appears Maks has discovered my trip to meet you."

Gillian had no chance to answer before the driver's door slammed open and Maks sprang out. Moving forward with speed, his attention so completely on Gillian, he did not hear his mother's greeting as he walked right by her.

The queen smiled, surprising Gillian, turning to watch as Maks swept Gillian into his arms and kissed her until she was breathless.

Deciding he knew the protocols best, Gillian went with it and kissed him back, letting her body relax into the man she loved. Once again in his arms, her worries for their future dissipated.

Eventually he pulled back, though he kept her close, facing him, as Maks's dark eyes searched her own with an intense expression she didn't understand. "How was your flight?"

"Fine."

"I did not expect you to have company." He still hadn't acknowledged his mother's presence.

"Me, either."

"Is it all right? Did she…" Maks looked over at his mother, his expression one Gillian could live the rest of her life without having directed at her. "She did not attempt to turn you off marrying me."

There was no question that *if* Oxana had tried that route, it would have led to a near irreparable schism with her son.

"I did nothing, Maks, but get to know the lovely woman you intend to marry."

They actually had spent some time talking like two new friends, before the queen had insisted Gillian take a nap for the remainder of the flight. Oxana had kindly woken Gillian in time to brush her hair and teeth in the jet's lavatory before landing, so she didn't feel so rumpled meeting Maks.

"If she said anything to upset you…" Again that look.

And it made Gillian feel badly. Oxana loved her son deeply. "She only wants your happiness, Maks."

"I am happy to be marrying you."

"And to be a father, I am sure," Oxana said smoothly.

Maks jolted, as if it had not occurred to him that his mother would learn the truth before he told her. Which made no sense. How could Maks have believed that Demyan would keep something that elemental from the queen?

Oxana was right. Maks wasn't thinking with his usual clarity.

Gillian shook her head. "It's fine. She's happy about the baby, too. Okay?"

Maks again searched Gillian's features, as if he was not sure he believed her before turning to examine his mother with the same questioning intensity.

The older woman frowned. "How can you doubt it?"

He did not answer, but turned back to Gillian.

She looked up into brown eyes that caught at her heart.

"She did not upset you?"

"I was surprised when I found her on the plane," Gillian deflected.

Unmistakable worry washed over Maks's features. "But you are not upset."

Grateful he'd used the present tense rather than the past, she was able to answer without prevaricating. "No."

"Very well."

"Maksim. Really." The hurt outrage in Oxana's tone rang sincerely. "You will have Gillian believing I am a monster."

Maks sighed, his expression showing guilt only a loving mother could engender.

He turned his face toward Oxana, but he kept his body in a protective stance around Gillian. "Of course not."

Incredibly, Oxana laughed, the sound soft and free somehow. "Oh, Maksim, I was so afraid I'd ruined your ability to love."

Maks went rigid. "Love is—"

"A tremendous blessing when the one who loves

practices selflessness rather than selfishness," Oxana interrupted in a very unroyal way.

Maks opened his mouth to respond, but Oxana shook her head. "I fear that between your father and I, you have only ever seen the selfish side of romantic love. Perhaps if you'd spent any time with the countess, you would have seen what selfless love is like."

"How can you say that woman—"

Oxana put her hand up, interrupting again. "She is more than *that woman,* Maksim. She is *the* woman, the one woman who offered your father love without strings and he took it. Selfishly."

"Mother."

"Come, this is no place for a discussion about our family's brokenness."

Gillian thought perhaps both Maks and Oxana should have considered that reality before this moment; this entire night had been a strange one.

Maks frowned and insisted, "Our family is not broken."

The queen merely smiled that enigmatic smile and walked toward the limousine. "Come, Maksim. Ivan can drive your car back to the palace."

"I wanted…"

"Gillian is too fatigued for a nighttime tour of the capital city. Come, Gillian. Bring my son with you." The imperious tone wasn't one Gillian would think of dismissing.

Thankfully Maks showed he was smart enough not to, either.

Soon, they were all ensconced in the limo, Maks's car in Ivan's care. Despite the roomy compartment, Maks kept Gillian so close she was practically sitting on his lap.

She didn't mind. Not a bit. The closeness, his constant touching, it all helped overcome that sense of despondency she'd been feeling on the plane.

Laying her head on his chest, Gillian snuggled in as she wouldn't have dreamed she could do in front of his very proper royal mother.

Once the car was moving, Oxana said, "Maksim, I am very displeased."

"I'm sorry to hear that, Mother, but I will marry Gillian."

"Of course you will. She's the mother of your child."

"She is *sérce moje*," he said with conviction.

"That is all well and good, Maksim, to say she is your heart. What she does not realize is that she *fills* your heart. Her reaction to my presence on her plane made that very clear."

"Mother," Maks warned.

Gillian didn't know what the queen was trying to prove, but whatever it was, Gillian was afraid it was going to end up breaking Gillian's heart all over again.

"Fine." Oxana crossed her arms in most unqueenly like fashion, a stubborn glint in her dark eyes. "You told me you love my son, Gillian."

"Yes," she croaked out.

Her feelings had been laid bare already. It shouldn't

hurt to have them dragged into the light right now, only
it did. Very much.

And she really wasn't sure why.

Oxana nodded, like she expected nothing less than
Gillian's agreement. Then she pressed, "Enough?"

"Yes." It didn't matter what Oxana meant, what Gillian loved Maks enough for.

She'd loved him enough *not* to go to him with news
of her pregnancy to protect him and his freedom. She
loved him enough for whatever it took to put his happiness above her own.

And then Gillian knew; this was the great power of
love he could not understand.

But she knew it was there and would never again
doubt the strength it could give her.

"Enough to give him his freedom after your child
is born and a sufficient period of time has passed?"
Oxana asked.

Gillian didn't hesitate. "Yes."

"No," Maks barked at the same time, his volume
much higher than hers, his conviction laced with desperation she didn't understand.

If she did not know better, she would think he was
the one unsure of *her* feelings for *him*.

He turned to her, his expression wounded in a way
she'd never expected to see. "You will not leave me."

"She knows that you are better off without her if you
do not love her." Oxana's eyes were filled with both certainty and compassion.

Maks sucked in a harsh breath. *"No."*

"Yes." Gillian felt the pain of that admission, but it wasn't greater than the strength of her love. "You deserve to find love, to live with the glorious knowledge that there is one person in this world whose happiness will always come ahead of your own."

"No. Damn it to hell! You are not leaving me." He turned a sulfuric glare on his mother. "If she leaves me, I will never forgive you."

The certainty in his tone left no room to question his absolute sincerity in the statement.

Oxana flinched, but she never looked away from her son's anger. "Why, Maksim? What would make you turn from your family so completely?"

"She is mine."

"And are you hers?" Oxana asked, her own voice sharp with pained censure.

Gillian understood only too well. King Fedir had never been hers, but Oxana had given the man her own heart and life.

He'd squandered both and never realized it, or if he had, did not care.

"Yes. I am hers." The ferocity in Maks's tone was matched by the way he pulled Gillian tighter into his body.

She squeaked.

He looked down at her, but did not relax his hold. "Are you all right?"

She nodded, completely lost for words in this conversation that seemed to be leading a direction she'd been absolutely sure no discussion between her and Maks could ever go.

The Rolls-Royce stopped and Oxana set a gimlet stare on her son. "You will give her the words. You will not hold *anything* back from a woman who loves you enough to give you your freedom for the sake of your happiness even knowing it will decimate her own heart finally and forever."

The queen got out of the car, walking toward the palace without looking back.

Tension vibrating off him like the aftershocks of an earthquake, Maks followed. Gillian went with them.

She had no choice. Maks had a hold of her and he wasn't letting go.

Full stop. Period.

Gillian barely noticed the austere beauty of the palace's architecture, or the opulence within. Her attention was fixed entirely on the man leading her across the massive foyer, up one side of a double marble staircase and down a long corridor.

He stopped when they'd gone into a room that could belong to no one but him with its masculine luxury.

He turned to face her. "Would you like a bath before bed?"

"Don't I have my own room?"

He shrugged. Like it didn't matter.

"I thought the idea wasn't to make a big splash in the media. Won't someone notice I'm sleeping in your room? That can't be appropriate, surely?"

"I am Crown Prince—no one will question me."

"The media don't have to question. They just have to report."

"Let them report it then."

"Maks! You're not thinking straight."

He stared down at her, his jaw taut with emotion she was beginning to think exceeded anything he'd ever admitted to. "I thought my mother would try to convince you to leave me."

"Why? You said she approved of me as your potential wife."

His paranoia was irrational, emotionally driven.

The concept blew her belief about their relationship straight into space. Because Maks claimed not to be motivated by emotion with her.

Had he been lying to himself and her?

"She went to meet you. She didn't tell me beforehand. That kind of subterfuge never ends well."

"She didn't do anything wrong, Maks."

"She suggested you leave me." The pained betrayal in his tone hurt Gillian's own heart.

But it made those champagne bubbles of hope start fizzing again too.

"Only after our child was guaranteed his or her place in the House of Yurkovich."

"Do you think that is all that matters to me?" he demanded, his eyes wounded. "Is it all that matters to you?"

"You know it isn't."

"Then why would you leave me?"

"So you can find love."

"I have already found love," he shouted, his entire body rigid with feeling he didn't seem able to keep inside anymore.

Emotion she had been utterly sure he didn't have inside of him. "You broke up with me."

"I should not have done."

Could it be that simple?

"You need heirs."

"I need you."

"You do?" she asked softly, her heart blossoming like a rose under the sun.

He stopped and stared at her. "*Koxána moja.* I live for you. My brain is clouded with thoughts of you. I forget my place in the middle of a meeting and find myself texting you while businessmen and politicians watch, believing I am contacting someone of more importance than them. It is the truth, but not in a way most would understand."

From his tone, it was obvious Maks wasn't truly understanding it himself.

"The prospect of you leaving me again fills me with dread." The intense feeling lacing his voice brought moisture stinging to her eyes. "What would you call it?"

"Love. I would call that love."

Could it be true?

He stared at her, his expression so dismayed it was almost comical. "I just called you my love."

"I didn't know that."

"I will teach you the words, so you can say them to our children."

"All right."

He dropped to his knees in front of her, his expression stricken. "I love you, more than duty, I love you. And I tried to deny it. There are no words for the depths of my sorrow at my own cowardice."

"You aren't a coward." Just a man who had been raised to believe that love was not meant for his future. "You didn't let your mind even consider the possibility."

And she'd refused to consider it, either. She'd been too afraid, too certain he couldn't love her.

But Oxana had known. Gillian shook her head at the inexplicable powers of loving mothers.

"No, do not shake your head. I *do* love you. I did not say it, but surely my actions pointed to it."

"I was shaking my head at your mother's intuition."

"My mother." Oh, the anger in his voice.

"She wanted you to admit your love—she never intended that I leave you."

"You are so sure."

"If you were feeling more rational, you would be, too."

"I am always rational."

"Except maybe when you are admitting for the first time that you are in love."

He opened his mouth, looked at her and then closed it again.

She smiled down at him. "I love you, with my whole heart."

"You loved me enough to let me go for my own benefit."

"Yes."

"Let us be clear on this. It will *never* be for my benefit for you to leave me."

"Okay."

He leaned down and kissed her stomach. "Our children will know nothing but the supreme power and joy of love."

"And making up, maybe." They were both too strong willed for them never to argue.

Maks gave her his most rakish grin. "I believe we have makeup sex to participate in now."

"We were arguing?" she asked.

"Oh, yes. You even threatened to leave me." His hands were already busy on her clothing, undoing a button here, sliding down a zipper there.

"Never again."

"Never again."

They made love for the first time with their love pouring between them in cascade after cascade of emotional bliss.

Later they cuddled in his huge bed and Maks whispered against her hair, "Say it again."

"I love you and I will never leave you."

"I love you, *sérce moje.*"

She thought she just might be able to live the rest of her life as his heart, so long as she lived in it.

And now she knew she did.

EPILOGUE

THE WEDDING ABOARD the luxury cruise liner was both beautiful and intimate.

Maks made sure Gillian's grandparents were there as well as both the king and queen of Volyarus. His cousin Demyan was his best man and Gillian's grandmother stood at her side as her matron of honor, tears tracking down weathered cheeks.

The State reception that followed was indeed not even a nine days wonder; Gillian's giving birth only six months later causing only marginally more of a blip on the media's radar.

But then that might have been because of the sensational wedding between Demyan and the long-lost granddaughter of Bartholomew Tanner from the original Yurkovich Tanner partnership.

Gillian thought there was something squirrelly about that wedding, but she was so wrapped up in her new baby and incandescent happiness married to the love of her life, she let the thought float away on the breeze of her own joy.

* * * * *

Mills & Boon® Hardback
July 2013

ROMANCE

His Most Exquisite Conquest	Emma Darcy
One Night Heir	Lucy Monroe
His Brand of Passion	Kate Hewitt
The Return of Her Past	Lindsay Armstrong
The Couple who Fooled the World	Maisey Yates
Proof of Their Sin	Dani Collins
In Petrakis's Power	Maggie Cox
A Shadow of Guilt	Abby Green
Once is Never Enough	Mira Lyn Kelly
The Unexpected Wedding Guest	Aimee Carson
A Cowboy To Come Home To	Donna Alward
How to Melt a Frozen Heart	Cara Colter
The Cattleman's Ready-Made Family	Michelle Douglas
Rancher to the Rescue	Jennifer Faye
What the Paparazzi Didn't See	Nicola Marsh
My Boyfriend and Other Enemies	Nikki Logan
The Gift of a Child	Sue MacKay
How to Resist a Heartbreaker	Louisa George

MEDICAL

Dr Dark and Far-Too Delicious	Carol Marinelli
Secrets of a Career Girl	Carol Marinelli
A Date with the Ice Princess	Kate Hardy
The Rebel Who Loved Her	Jennifer Taylor

Mills & Boon® Large Print

July 2013

ROMANCE

HISTORICAL

MEDICAL

ROMANCE

The Billionaire's Trophy	Lynne Graham
Prince of Secrets	Lucy Monroe
A Royal Without Rules	Caitlin Crews
A Deal with Di Capua	Cathy Williams
Imprisoned by a Vow	Annie West
Duty At What Cost?	Michelle Conder
The Rings that Bind	Michelle Smart
An Inheritance of Shame	Kate Hewitt
Faking It to Making It	Ally Blake
Girl Least Likely to Marry	Amy Andrews
The Cowboy She Couldn't Forget	Patricia Thayer
A Marriage Made in Italy	Rebecca Winters
Miracle in Bellaroo Creek	Barbara Hannay
The Courage To Say Yes	Barbara Wallace
All Bets Are On	Charlotte Phillips
Last-Minute Bridesmaid	Nina Harrington
Daring to Date Dr Celebrity	Emily Forbes
Resisting the New Doc In Town	Lucy Clark

MEDICAL

Miracle on Kaimotu Island	Marion Lennox
Always the Hero	Alison Roberts
The Maverick Doctor and Miss Prim	Scarlet Wilson
About That Night...	Scarlet Wilson

Mills & Boon® Large Print
August 2013

ROMANCE

Master of her Virtue	Miranda Lee
The Cost of her Innocence	Jacqueline Baird
A Taste of the Forbidden	Carole Mortimer
Count Valieri's Prisoner	Sara Craven
The Merciless Travis Wilde	Sandra Marton
A Game with One Winner	Lynn Raye Harris
Heir to a Desert Legacy	Maisey Yates
Sparks Fly with the Billionaire	Marion Lennox
A Daddy for Her Sons	Raye Morgan
Along Came Twins...	Rebecca Winters
An Accidental Family	Ami Weaver

HISTORICAL

The Dissolute Duke	Sophia James
His Unusual Governess	Anne Herries
An Ideal Husband?	Michelle Styles
At the Highlander's Mercy	Terri Brisbin
The Rake to Redeem Her	Julia Justiss

MEDICAL

The Brooding Doc's Redemption	Kate Hardy
An Inescapable Temptation	Scarlet Wilson
Revealing The Real Dr Robinson	Dianne Drake
The Rebel and Miss Jones	Annie Claydon
The Son that Changed his Life	Jennifer Taylor
Swallowbrook's Wedding of the Year	Abigail Gordon